The Neptun

Ronald Bassett

© Ronald Bassett 1979

Ronald Bassett has asserted his rights under the Copyright, Design and Patents Act, 1988, to be identified as the author of this work.

First published in 1979 by Macmillan London Ltd.

This edition published in 2015 by Endeavour Press Ltd.

Table of Contents

Author's Foreword — 5

One — 11

Two — 23

Three — 35

Four — 46

Five — 63

Six — 80

Seven — 96

Eight — 109

Nine — 122

Glossary of Naval Lower-deck Terminology and Technical Terms — 134

Author's Foreword

In 1939 there was probably no strategist in the world capable of envisaging, far less planning, an invasion landing on the scale achieved against the coast of Normandy in June 1944. If any pre-war plans were formulated, the only yardsticks against which they could have been measured were the heroic but costly failure of the Dardanelles, the limited success of Zeebrugge and the total failure of Ostend in 1918 — the latter two operations being little more than commando raids. None was encouraging, and the lessons subsequently learned at St Nazaire and Dieppe could have inspired little confidence in an ability to land successfully an invasion army on a fortified shore.

In any conflict between a land monster and a sea monster there is, to some extent, a stalemate. To reach a conclusion either the elephant or the whale must enter into the other's habitat, with all that this implies. The German attempt took the form of a prolonged and intensive U-boat campaign which almost succeeded. Britain possessed the world's most powerful navy but, alone, her land forces could not nearly match the full strength of the Axis armies. Moreover, the Royal Navy was already fully stretched in blockading enemy-occupied Europe, provisioning overseas theatres, and in maintaining the convoy lifelines without which Britain and, incidentally, the Irish Republic would have starved within weeks. Even after the entry of the United States into the war only two per cent of convoy escorts were American, and even on D-Day 1944 the bombarding warships, landing ships, assault and support craft were overwhelmingly British. The whale had come ashore, and this time it won.

The preponderance of British over American ships in the Atlantic and in European waters was not the result of any American evasion of responsibility but stemmed from the fact that the Allies' naval priorities differed. The United States navy had deployed almost all its strength in the Pacific, which Admiral Ernest King, the American C-in-C considered to be the more important theatre and where, indeed, there were British interests. King, also, was an Anglophobe who did not wish to see

American warships operating under overall British command, which was inevitable if they were sent to Europe. 'I fought under the goddam' British in the First World War,' he said, 'and if I can help it, no ships of mine will fight under them again.' The warships and invasion craft that did cross the Atlantic were conceded reluctantly; they fought magnificently and erased completely any feelings of resentment there might have been among their British counterparts.

In the beginning, however, there was nothing that resembled an invasion fleet. The Royal Navy had a small number of prototype motorized landing craft, both steel and wooden, some laid down as early as 1926, others as late as 1939. The largest were of twenty tons displacement unladen and accommodated either 100 men or one twelve-ton tank. Inadequate and few in number though they were, these were the forerunners of a vast armada of assault vessels of every conceivable size, type and purpose such as the world had never seen, nor will ever see again.

Planning a major invasion which had to succeed at the first attempt was like fighting a multi-headed hydra. It seemed that solving one problem only meant that two more problems revealed themselves. There was no starting-point, an intimidating multitude of imponderables, and there were to be many trials and many errors before a discernible pattern began to emerge.

The original distinction between a landing ship and a landing craft, apart from size, was that the first was not required to beach but could make lengthy sea voyages under its own power, while the second, which was required to beach, would be carried or towed, to be released only in proximity to the point of landing. This distinction, however, became blurred and finally disappeared; landing ships did beach and many types of landing craft were capable of making long sea passages unaccompanied. Non-beaching ships were invariably mercantile conversions and included train ferries, tankers, passenger and cargo liners; ships that beached were designed and purpose-built during the war years.

Whatever their size or design, however, landing ships and craft were only carriers of men and materials. They were 'soft-skinned', had little fighting capability and, before they could approach an enemy shore, the enemy's defences had to be subjected to bombardment or bombing and the sky cleared of enemy aircraft. The navy had battleships, monitors, cruisers and destroyers, and there would be adequate air cover, but pre-assault bombardments cannot be prolonged or the element of surprise begins to drain and the enemy has time to deploy his own resources. Additionally, bombardments from relatively long range are often less effective than is hoped; defence positions survive and can inflict punishing casualties when the barrage is lifted. It was most necessary, therefore, to provide armed support vessels, of shallow draft, that could precede or accompany the landing operation, and beach if necessary, to engage still-active gun emplacements, tanks, troops and possibly aircraft.

Already well proven in other theatres were the larger tank landing craft — LCT(L), or Landing Craft Tank Large. These varied in detail, but were between 200 and 350 tons unladen and about 170 feet in length, with engine room, crew quarters and bridge structure aft, and a long forward well-deck from which tanks or other vehicles could be discharged via a hinged ramp in the bows. The design was box-like and unsophisticated, so that they could be assembled by steel constructors with little or no ship-building experience. Crew facilities were primitive because, initially, it was thought that crews would be embarked for periods of only a few days, living normally ashore or in accommodation vessels. In this respect the planners were mistaken. Crews lived aboard for many months which occasionally stretched into years, and took their ungainly craft on ocean passages that had never been considered possible. It was also the sturdy LCT(L) design that formed the basis for two classes of close support craft — the Landing Craft Flak and the Landing Craft Gun.

There was a number of variants of these, but structural modifications were basically similar. The bow ramp was removed, although the bows remained clumsily square, and the after bridge structure was enlarged. More radically, the entire tank deck was overlaid by 3/8-inch armour plate to provide, below accommodation for gun-crews — a company of Royal Marines — magazine, galley, ablution space and a diminutive wardroom, and, above, a sizeable gun deck. The existing naval crew's quarters aft remained unchanged.

Initially, two LCTs were experimentally converted, one equipped with a main armament of two twin four-inch gun turrets, controlled by an RDF High Angle Director Control Tower abaft the bridge, the other with eight single two-pounder guns and four 20-mm guns. Opinion was divided as to whether heavy or light armament was more suitable for close support purposes.

Both prototypes — LCF1 and LCF2 — were successful. The heavier-gunned LCF1 established the pattern for the LCG, intended for inshore bombardment (although later versions were fitted with two 4.7-inch guns, ex-destroyers) while LCF2 introduced the gun-bristling LCF series which, paradoxically, was to be employed almost exclusively in close support fighting and almost never in an anti-aircraft role.

Almost by definition the task of the LCF and LCG was hazardous. With negligible armour — and in the LCFs the crews were openly exposed — they were required to run the gauntlet of enemy guns, sometimes of immense calibre and protected by reinforced concrete bunkers and pillboxes, at point-blank range. LCF2, the prototype, was lost in 1942, and an LCF and two LCGs in 1943. Not unpredictably, the Normandy landings exacted the biggest toll of five LCFs and five LCGs, most of them during the immediate post-landing period when both types were engaged in defending the beachhead and its vast congestion of shipping against seaward attacks by midget submarines, E-boats, one-man torpedoes and radio-controlled explosive motor-boats. One of the casualties at this time was the doyen of the support craft force, LCF1, torpedoed and utterly obliterated by a midget submarine only yards from the author's own vessel, LCF21, which picked up one survivor from a crew of seventy-five.

Millions of words have been written about the Normandy landings but, after the assault phase of the first few days, interest was inevitably focused on the fortunes of the Allied forces pushing inland, on the battles for St Lo, Caen, and the Cherbourg peninsula; it was perhaps overlooked that there was still a battle being fought in the Channel approaches, to the rear and on both flanks of the beachhead, to ensure that the German navy did not disrupt the flow of supplies and reinforcements that, vitally, must match the corresponding build-up of the enemy. It was fortuitous that several new German weapons were not yet being produced in sufficient numbers to be operationally decisive, but neither could they be ignored, and the enemy naval forces sallying from Brest, St Nazaire, Le Havre and Cherbourg did not lack courage or determination. While destroyers and aircraft scoured the more distant waters, it was a tired and unsung force of LCFs, LCGs and similar small ships that formed the Trout Line — the long, anchored cordon to seaward — from every dusk to dawn, to wait in darkness and silence for the night's infiltrators. They had fulfilled the task for which they had come to Normandy, the assault on the beaches, and now they were expendable.

One

Leading Signalman Lobby Ludd, D/JX245613, chose the least muddy area of Govan pavement upon which to deposit his hammock and kitbag and fumbled again for his drafting instructions. From the moment they had been given to him at Devonport he had assumed that the designation LCF49 was not a ship's name but a dockyard job number that might hide the identity of anything from a corvette to an aircraft carrier. Whatever the ship was, he knew, it had not yet been commissioned. 'LCF' probably indicated the builder — such as Lower Clydebank Fairfield. In fact, that was probably exactly what it was. Fairfield had built the battleships Queen Elizabeth, Valiant, Warspite, Howe, the Renown, carriers, cruisers, destroyers. The truck that had brought him from Glasgow Central weaved past several docked warships, newly built or building among giant cranes, the flare of acetylene and the deafening tattoo of riveting hammers, but did not halt. When at last it did, the shabby little jetty, scattered with debris and deserted of life, did not seem capable of accommodating anything more than a pair of Corporation buses. There was nothing in sight that slightly resembled a warship.

It was beginning to rain. Inside a grimy little gatehouse two able seamen stared morosely at a stove that glowed a dull red, their hands thrust deeply into oilskin pockets. 'Have you two blokes seen anything of an LCF Forty-nine?' Lobby asked. It was obviously the wrong dock.

There was a silence, then one of the seamen sighed deeply. 'We've seen it, mate,' he nodded. 'Too bleedin' true, we've seen it. It's a Landing Craft Flak, and we're the soddin' advance party. Only it ain't a ship. It's a bleedin' disaster.' He glared at the badge on Lobby Ludd's arm. 'A bunting-tosser? Shave off. We ain't going ter 'ave a flag, are we?' He turned to his companion. 'Perk, we're going ter 'ave a flag.' Perk seemed totally unmoved. He hawked and spat on the stove, which sizzled.

'Landing Craft Flak?' Lobby Ludd speculated. 'What's that, for Chrissake?' The seaman sighed again. 'Well may yer ask, mate. Yer can't describe an LCF. Yer've got ter see it, and when yer see it yer don't believe it. There ain't no such thing.' Lobby Ludd stared through the small dirty window at the rain beyond, trying to formulate a mental picture of a ship that was a bleedin' disaster. 'Is the ship's office manned?' He supposed he ought to report his arrival to someone.

'Ship's office?' The other's eyes widened. 'Did yer 'ear that, Perk? Is the ship's office manned?' He snorted. 'The only soddin' thing that's open is the bilges in the mess-deck, mate. Wide open. The bleedin' deck's flooded. The galley ain't workin' 'cause there's no oil, an' there's no rations an' no mess-traps. We've got tickets ter eat in the Mission ter bleedin' Seamen. Yer can 'ave soup or beans on toast, an' a bloke tells yer about Jesus.' He shuddered. 'Roll on my soddin' twelve.'

'There's someone on board, ain't there? I mean, who's in charge?'

'There's me an' Perk, an' the First Lieutenant — a one-ringer named Summers who thinks he's soddin' Noel Coward in a war film — '

'This' — interrupted Perk bitterly, unable to suppress his indignation any longer — 'is our bleedin' stand easy. Yer've got ter come ashore ter git warm. We oughter complain, only there ain't nobody ter soddin' complain to.'

Lobby Ludd shrugged. 'Yer shouldn't 'ave bleedin' joined. Don't yer know there's thousands o' pongoes in Africa, fighting in the desert, just so's you can 'ave beans on toast?' Both seamen frowned at the stove. Perk sniffed. 'They've got soddin' palm-trees, ain't they?' He fastened the neck of his oilskin: 'You coming, Walt?'

They emerged into the drizzling rain, crossed rusting railway lines and a stretch of mud scattered with weeds and corroding scrap, then halted at the lip of the jetty. 'She was built in a field,' Perk said, 'in parts, then stuck tergether. I reckon she's sitting on the bottom. She'll never bleedin' float.'

The object of his comment had earlier been hidden from view because the water in the basin was low, and only the upper few feet of the masthead showed above the jetty. The vessel was 190 feet long, flush-decked, with squared, puntshaped bows and a heavy kedge-anchor hung from the stern. A box-like wheel-house, well aft, supported an open bridge, and there was an upright narrow funnel accommodating diesel exhausts. On the small after-deck there was just space for a capstan, hawser drum, a dinghy slung from davits and, in mid-deck, a circular hatch like a dustbin lid that opened to the sky. There was a similar engine-room hatch, a covered ladder descending to the wardroom, and two other hatches farther forward. Of greater curiosity, however, was the vessel's armament. The long fore-deck mounted four two-pounder pom-poms and eight 20-mm Oerlikons, each gun surrounded by a circular steel coaming two feet high and seeming to offer protection only to the gun-crews' below-knees. Angular, ill-balanced, the ship's every proportion was discordant to the eye and a travesty of maritime design. LCF49 sat squatly and sulkily in the dirty basin, and Lobby Ludd decided that he had seen nothing uglier since Fulham Gasworks. 'Christ,' he gritted, and his heart sank. 'It ain't true.'

'Jes' wait till they open the caisson,' Walt gloated, 'and let the bleedin' water in. Then yer'll see. She ain't even soddin' rain-proof. I'm going to be standing near the dinghy, mate.'

Sub-Lieutenant David Summers, RNVR, emerged from the wardroom hatch. He was young, slight and dark, his cap-badge was very new, and he delicately avoided the puddles on the deck. In a gloved hand he carried a small red notebook into which, at frequent intervals, he pencilled brief notes, and, when he spoke, his clipped voice had the slightest of Welsh accents.

'Perkins and Walters,' he glared. 'Stand easy is for ten minutes, not forty-five. And take your hands out of your pockets.'

'We was delayed, sir,' Perk apologized, 'bringing the new draft aboard. We've got a killick bunting-tosser, and we didn't think yer'd want 'im lorst.'

'It looks like there's been a mistake, sir,' Lobby Ludd suggested. 'I can't think why yer'd want a leading signalman on a thing like this. I mean, it ain't as if it's going ter sea. If yer want to send signals, yer can walk down ter the phone box.' He glanced around the basin. 'Who'm I supposed ter send signals to? The steam laundry in Paisley Road?' Sub-Lieutenant Summers placed his hands behind his back and narrowed his eyes. 'Do you realize that ships like this have gone to the Mediterranean, and even crossed the Atlantic? Sicily, Reggio, Salerno, Anzio ... ' He spoke the names in a manner that suggested an acquaintance with all of them. 'It's men that make a ship what it is — seamanship, alertness, determination. The Glowworm wasn't much bigger than this, but she engaged the Hipper — ' From behind him, Perk made an odd choking noise, and Summers whirled, but the seaman's face was innocent.

Summers turned his attention to Lobby Ludd's papers. 'From Royal Naval Barracks, Devonport. I suppose you've had some operational experience, Ludd?' Lobby Ludd considered. 'Well, not like all them places you've been, sir. I did a spell in the destroyer Virtue, in the Arctic, but it was a cock-up. We only sunk one U-boat, and we lost a destroyer, a corvette and two trawlers, then got tin-fished ourselves. I clewed up with two broken legs. Then I was in the cruiser Daemon, Med. Fleet. We rammed a U-boat and then lost a screw, but we did pick up two thousand survivors from the Susquehanna. O' course, it weren't nothing like fighting the Hipper.' He regarded Summers admiringly. 'I bet that was blood an' snot. Who fired first, sir — you or the Hipper?' Sub-Lieutenant Summers looked at his watch, then referred to his red notebook. 'Perkins, Walters — I want that water cleared from the after mess-deck, or you don't secure until it is.'

'We've been balin' out water all day, sir,' Walt said, 'and it don't make a spit o' difference. Perk and me reckon there's an 'ole. If yer've noticed, sir, the water on the inside always stays the same as the water on the outside. We measured it through the scuttle wi' a squeegee. Perk and me reckon we're on a slope — '

'I don't care a damn what you reckon, Walters,' Summers snorted. 'I haven't seen the pair of you lift three buckets of water out of that hatch since you started.' He braced himself. 'Let me tell you something, Walters. And you, Perkins. Seven days from now, this ship must be ready for sea. The rest of the ship's company joins tomorrow, and the commanding officer on the following day. I intend to hand over a fighting ship. You, Ludd' — he turned — 'have obviously been sent in advance for an important reason. Tomorrow is the first day of our commission, and I shall want colours hoisted at oh-eight-double-oh. You will find all the flags and pennants piled on the bridge.' He returned to Perkins and Walters. 'You two had better smarten up. This might not be a fleet destroyer but, by God, I'll see that it's just as efficient. I want to see some effort.'

'The trouble is, sir,' Perk complained, 'there ain't nowhere ter sit. I was sayin' ter Walt, if yer sit on the mess-stool yer've got yer feet in the water, unless yer lie down — '

Summers consulted his notebook. 'And as from tomorrow there will be a quartermaster at the gang-plank who will check visitors, attend to the moorings, and pipe routine orders. You Perkins, will have the forenoon watch. You will be responsible for security.'

Perk was interested. 'Will I have a gun, sir?' he asked hopefully.

'A gun?' Summers choked. 'Good God, I wouldn't trust you with a gun, Perkins, if there were German stormtroopers marching through the dockyard gate. You will wear number threes, salute all officers, challenge civilians, and try to look seamanlike. Challenging civilians does not mean shouting ribaldries at passing women.'

'Shave off,' Perk said, when Summers was beyond earshot. 'I can see we're goin' ter 'ave trouble with 'im. Yer'd think, on active service, there'd be a sort o' bond between officers an' men, wouldn't yer?'

*

Lobby Ludd eased himself from his hammock at 0730, cursed as his bare feet met the wet deck, and dressed, shivering. Perk and Walt were still sleeping soundly, and he climbed to the upper deck. It was still only half light, the surrounding jetties desolate and quiet, with masts and cranes starkly latticed against a grey sky. There would be a hot stove, he knew, in the gate house, and he debated whether he should take the mess-kettle to brew tea, but decided there would be insufficient time. He blew on his fingers and went to the bridge.

Yesterday, on the deck, there had been a huge mound of sodden flags and pennants that he had sorted, rolled, and placed in their respective flag-locker pigeon-holes. He had found an ensign, and now he bent it on to the halyard, then looked at his watch. In a few more minutes LCF49 would be a commissioned ship of His Majesty's Navy.

He waited. It was soddin' cold and he wished he had worn an oilskin. He glanced at his watch again. 0800. He hoisted the ensign to the mast-head, secured the halyard and descended the bridge ladder. Perk had appeared with the mess-kettle, swollen-eyed and wearing a duffel-coat over a green-and-white striped football shirt. 'Bleedin' brass monkeys,' he observed. 'I'm goin' ter wet the tea, mate. There's only two cups, but Walt ain't broke surface yet. After, we'll amble down ter the Mission ter Seamen, fer breakfus'.'

There was a distant, anguished shout, and both turned. Sub-Lieutenant Summers had emerged from the wardroom hatch and was advancing with a raised fist and a shocked face. 'Ludd!' he roared. 'For God's sake! You've hoisted the ensign!'

15

'That's right, sir,' Lobby Ludd agreed. 'Now the Germans can watch out. It's the beginning o' the end.'

'Take it down,' Summers ordered.

Lobby Ludd stared. 'Take it down, sir? I jes' put it up.'

'Don't you realize, Ludd,' the Sub-Lieutenant gritted, 'that the commissioning of a naval warship is a distinguished occasion, and that there's a traditional ceremony associated with raising the colours? What the hell do you suppose the first entry in the log will be? "Ludd pulled up flag, Perkins made tea"?' Then he froze. 'What the blazes are you wearing, Perkins? You're supposed to be the quartermaster.'

Perkins winced. 'Glasgow Rangers, sir — '

Summers clenched his eyes and drew a shuddering breath, fighting for composure. Then he spoke very deliberately. 'All right, Perkins. Go below for your cap and return immediately without the kettle. Ludd — lower the ensign, then wait. We shall raise the colours again, and we shall do it in accordance with Admiralty Instructions. You will hoist slowly, Perkins will pipe, and I shall salute. Is that absolutely clear?'

Followed by Summers, Lobby Ludd returned to the bridge and lowered the ensign. The Sub-Lieutenant stood to attention and Perkins reappeared, wearing a cap. 'I couldn't find mine, sir,' he reported, 'but I borrered Walt's. It's a bit big.'

'Shut up,' Summers ordered. 'Have you got your bosun's pipe?'

Perk shook his head. 'Christ, I ain't 'ad one of them fer years. Not since' — he considered — 'I jes' can't think when I last 'ad one — '

Sub-Lieutenant Summers swallowed hard. He had paled.

'Don't worry, sir,' Perk assured him, 'I'll whistle. I can whistle pretty good.'

'Ludd,' Summers hissed, 'hoist the colours.' He lifted a gloved hand in salute. Perk inserted his thumbs into his mouth and emitted a piercing shrill that halted several passing dockyard workers in their tracks. The ensign climbed to the masthead for the second time. Walt clambered from the after hatch carrying the mess-kettle and wearing a balaclava helmet. 'Perk!' he yelled. 'What about the bleedin' tea, then? Do I 'ave ter do everythin'? And where's my soddin' 'at?'

*

The second detachment of the ship's company arrived in several trucks in the late forenoon — a coxswain and a further four able seamen, an engine-room artificer and two stokers, an ordnance artificer, a wireman, a telegraphist and a sick-berth attendant. Aboard, they surveyed their surroundings with, a mutual lack of enthusiasm, and Sub-Lieutenant Summers mustered them on the fore-deck.

'I have not been impressed,' he said, pacing slowly with hands behind back, 'with the quality of those ratings who have joined this ship so far, but I intend to have an efficient ship, and I intend to start now — '

'Shave off,' Walt muttered. 'It's the bleedin' Fightin' Navy bit again — '

'Dress of the day for quartermasters and communications ratings will be number three blue suits. Hands will muster daily at 0815 and 1315. Men working part of ship may wear clean overalls. Caps will be worn at all times, and there will be no smoking during working hours. The daily and Sunday routines will be posted on the mess-deck. Subject to confirmation by the commanding officer, who arrives tomorrow, I will see requestmen and defaulters daily, and inspect libertymen.' He paused. 'And until further notice Leading Signalman Ludd will be ship's postman.'

'Postman?' Lobby Ludd was incensed 'Me a soddin' postman?'

'And since he is the senior rating in the after mess,' Summers resumed, 'he will shake all hands at oh-six-thirty — and that means every morning.'

'Six-thirty?' Perk scowled. 'It's the middle of the bleedin' night.'

The Sub-Lieutenant referred to his notebook. 'We shall take on fuel from a lighter alongside this afternoon and, meanwhile, storing will continue. When oiling is completed, the generator will be started and we will disconnect shore powerlines. Tomorrow we shall be proceeding to the ammunition jetty.' He regarded them all grimly. 'There will then follow a strenuous period of working-up — engine trials, degaussing, compass-swinging, and general drill — to achieve a maximum state of proficiency before embarking a company of Royal Marine gun-crews, including two officers. Then, after an intensive programme of gunnery shoots, the ship will proceed to a yet unspecified destination to take her place with the Fleet.' He drew a deep breath. 'Are there any questions?'

'Shave off,' Walt marvelled.

*

Sub-Lieutenant Summers had been standing at the compass platform, polished feet astride, for several minutes, watching the crates and sacks being piled on the fore-deck below, when he became aware that he had been joined, in silence, by another officer. The newcomer was of middle height, of indeterminate age but with fair hair greying at the temples and a weather-tanned face that was badly shaven. He wore a shabby raincoat and an equally shabby cap, and the toes of his shoes were scuffed. He chewed on the stub of a cigarette.

'Ah,' Summers said, uncertain.

The other nodded agreeably. 'You must be Summers. I'm Turk, your new CO.'

Summers snapped to attention and executed an immaculate salute. 'Welcome aboard, sir.' Turk's blue eyes were mildly surprised, but he touched the peak of his cap. 'You seem to have everything well organized, Number One, but you should have a spring as well as forward and aft ropes. And the kedge needs winching in two or three feet; it's hanging like a Jew's bollock.'

Summers flushed. 'I'll see to it right away, sir — '

'Not now, Number One. Don't get excited,' Lieutenant Samuel Turk, RNR, sometime deep-sea trawler skipper from Lowestoft, took a fresh cigarette from a crumpled packet. 'Suppose you show me around?'

'Of course, sir. Delighted. If you'd like to come down to the wardroom — I've got a couple of hands unpacking our chinaware, glass and linen — '

'The after mess-deck first,' Turk said. 'Then the engine-room.'

'Of course, sir,' the Sub-Lieutenant agreed. 'We're not quite ship-shape yet, as you'll see.' He was unsure whether to lead or follow his superior, but they reached the after-deck and then descended the vertical steel ladder to the gloomy seamen's mess.

'Good God,' Turk frowned. 'What's all this water? And why are the bilges uncovered? You haven't got men living down here, have you?'

'Well — yes, sir. I've had a couple of men baling out, but you know what these seamen are like, and there have been other priorities — '

'Baling out? With buckets?' Turk stooped to peer under an open deck-plate, then walked to the scuttle. 'You're a bloody fool, Summers. You could bale this out until doomsday, and never shift it. It's a defective seam in the bottom, I'd say. The water level inboard is the same as that in the basin. Can't you bloody well see that? And what do you mean, there've been other priorities?' He halted Summer's flustered response with a wave of a hand. 'Now listen. Pipe all hands to take kitbags and hammocks to the forward mess-deck. Nobody will mess in this pigsty until it's been drained and dried. Then find the dockyard superintendent and tell him we want a pump and a hot-air blower aboard now. I mean now. I don't intend to sign any bloody acceptance papers until that riveting has been made good — and we're slipping tomorrow, so I don't care if he's working all damn night. When you've done that, report back to me.' The Sub-Lieutenant hesitated, but there was something in Turk's mild expression that forbade argument. 'Well — move, Number One,' Turk said quietly, and Summers moved.

When he returned, Turk was in the engine-room, having already closely inspected the two big Paxman Ricardo diesel motors, the generator, switchboard and batteries, and was now debating with the ERA the probability of engine noise drowning any voice-pipe communication with the bridge. 'Orders for rev-speed alterations will have to be made by bell.' he decided. 'The First Lieutenant will devise a bell code.' Summers made a hurried entry in his notebook.

They reached the galley. 'Not exactly generous for seventy-five men,' Turk observed, then turned. 'But why is the stove cold, Number One? Why isn't someone cooking?' He looked at his watch.

Summers chuckled apologetically. 'Ah — there's been no oil, sir. We only fuelled yesterday afternoon, and we haven't got around — '

'Fuel? But you don't have to fuel the ship to light a bloody galley stove! How the hell have the hands been eating?'

'In the Mission to Seamen — '

Turk glared. 'Baked beans, spam and margerine? Sod it, Summers, the men don't expect four-star catering, but they need soups, bangers and piles of mash, meat puddings, all the bread they can eat, plenty of strong tea. If there's one thing above all else that's important to any ship's company, it's adequate hot food — and it should have been your first responsibility. And you hadn't got around to it?' He reached for the stove's oil valve. 'We'll get around to it now. Soak a handful of waste in oil, light it, then toss it in here. That's right — take those bloody gloves off. Then tell the coxswain to detail a couple of men to peeling spuds — plenty — break out a dozen tins of meat and veg, and we'll follow that with pears and custard. Can you make custard, Number One? Well, you're going to bloody well learn.'

*

Within an hour of Lieutenant Turk's arrival a number of things were beginning to happen. The First Lieutenant strode about purposefully, tapping things and trying door-clips. The after section of the bilges was being pumped, a dockyard welder and his mate were waiting to descend, and a hot-air blower was rigged. There was a trickle of smoke from the galley chimney. Clothes lines had disappeared from the magazine, the generator was humming, there was lighting and power, hot water in the bathroom, and the latrines flushed. Lobby Ludd rigged his twelve-inch signal lamp, the telegraphist put his batteries on charge, the seamen were making up heaving-lines, the wireman made mysterious tests with a voltmeter and the ordnance artificer peered speculatively into gun-breeches, sucking his teeth. Perk had discovered that the electric fires functioned in the forward mess-deck, and told Walt.

The sick-berth attendant wandered aimlessly until Lieutenant Turk asked him if he had ever used a scalpel and, receiving a startled affirmative, ordered him to open twelve tins of meat and veg and give the contents a shock on the galley stove, slice three loaves and mash the spuds.

At 1400 Sub-Lieutenant Summers had just congratulated himself on having successfully achieved the winching-in of the kedge, which the coxswain competently supervised, when Turk emerged from his cabin. He wore his shabby cap as if it had been thrown at him from six yards, a muffler around his neck, and tartan carpet-slippers. 'Number One,' he ordered, 'start main engines, stand by the hands to cast off, then join me on the bridge. Coxswain on the wheel.' He swung up the bridge ladder. 'We'll run down to Gourock to take on that ammunition. It'll take you about three hours.'

Summers swallowed. 'Take me, sir?' But Turk was beyond hearing.

Minutes later Summers went to the bridge, deciding that he had misunderstood Turk. The engines were throbbing and the deck vibrated underfoot. Leading Signalman Ludd had hoisted the ship's pennants and was gazing at the sky with oddly intent interest. Turk smoking a cigarette, waited with an elbow on the wheel-house voice-pipe. Summers waited. The voice of Able Seaman Walters came distinctly from the deck below. 'Watch out, Perk. If yer 'ear an 'orrible crunching noise, jump fer the Bleedin 'jetty.'

Turk frowned. 'Well, come on, Number One. We haven't got all bloody day.' He changed elbows.

'You mean — ?' It was inconceivable. 'You mean you want me to take the ship down the Clyde?'

'If you know of a quicker way to Gourock, Number One, I'd like to bloody know it.' Turk sighed. 'Look — I'll give you a start. Let go forward. Let go aft. Slow ahead starboard.'

'Let go forward, let go aft,' Summers began.

'Don't bloody well tell me, Number One!' Turk exploded. 'Tell them!'

Summers cupped his hands around his mouth. 'Let go forward, let go aft!' he shouted, then sprang for the voice-pipe. 'Slow ahead starboard!'

'The coxswain isn't deaf,' Turk said. 'Now slow ahead port.'

'That entrance is very narrow, sir.' The First Lieutenant wetted his lips. There was a widening gap between ship and jetty, and a throng of dockyard workers had gathered to watch. 'Narrow?' Turk gritted. 'A bloody battleship could go through there.' He fumbled for a fresh cigarette.

LCF49 negotiated the basin entrance with sixty feet to spare on one beam but only five on the other. Lobby Ludd closed his eyes. 'Very daring,' Turk nodded. 'Now try to miss that new frigate on the port side, Number One. You won't be very popular with her commander if you take away all her boats and davits.' Lobby Ludd closed his eyes again.

'Shave off.' Perk groaned. 'I jes' remembered. My lifebelt's at the bottom o' my soddin' kitbag. Yer ain't going below, are yer, Walt?'

'No, I bleedin' ain't, mate,' Walt assured him. 'There was a bloke on the Titanic what went below fer 'is soddin' lifebelt. He's still lookin' fer it.'

The twenty miles of Clyde between Govan and Gourock were the most harrowing of Sub-Lieutenant Summers's young life and undoubtedly everyone else's except the engine-room hands, blissfully in ignorance. By the time the Gourock sheds were in sight even Lieutenant Turk's calm had begun to fray.

'All right, Number One,' he heaved. 'I'll take her alongside. Those look like mines piled on the jetty. Tempting bloody Providence is one thing, but kicking it in the teeth is something else.' He lit his fourteenth cigarette. 'I don't think we scraped that dredger off Erskine; if we did, the Glasgow Port Authority will let us know. You missed the workmen's ferry by a clear yard, even if you were in the wrong bloody fairway and as for that Excise launch, well, if it comes to anything, you'll have to say they were looking the wrong way. It didn't sink, anyway.' He loosened his muffler. 'Apart from that, Number One, it was very exciting — but for Christ's sake try to remember that ships don't have bloody brakes.'

'There oughter be a Society fer the Prevention o' Cruelty ter bleedin' Matelots,' Lobby Ludd said, regaining the mess-deck. 'And tomorrer oughter be a day o' prayer.'

'I'm asking fer a soddin' transfer, mate,' Perk decided. 'Something safe, like human bleedin' torpedoes.' He was peering into the mess-deck mirror. 'I thought so. I'm going soddin' white.'

From the open hatch the quartermaster's pipe squealed. 'Hands to muster on the upper deck. Stand by to take on ammunition.'

'That's what yer call a death knell,' Walt sniffed. 'After this we're goin' ter be a floatin' bomb.'

Two

Hundreds of boxes of two-pounder and 20-mm ammunition were net-slung from the Gourock jetty, with .303 ball, detonators, pistol flares and smoke floats, piled on the fore-deck and then lowered into the steel cavern of the magazine to be stowed in racks. There was a crude, see-saw hoist, intended to facilitate raising the heavy boxes from below but which offered little help in lowering them. When the sick-berth attendant had bandaged a number of bloodied fingers, the hoist was abandoned, and the men resigned themselves to several hours of primitive, exhausting labour. All men, Lieutenant Turk ordered, except SBA Peach, who, until the arrival of two cooks with the Royal Marine detachment, would be responsible for victualling. Since the alternative, had it been offered, was less attractive, SBA Peach did not seriously demur. True, his first offering, M&V — meat and veg, more usually referred to as Muzzle Velocity — had fallen short of excellence because, unable to find any salt, he had boiled the potatoes in brine. The crew had been blasphemous. Tonight there would be train smash — tinned tomatoes and bacon — which even Peach would find difficult to spoil. Meanwhile, Lieutenant Turk peeled off his jacket, which shocked Summers, who had firm ideas about the status of officers. 'All right, Number One,' Turk grunted, 'take your finger out, or it'll be bloody dark before we've finished.'

It was indeed dark before they finished. 'The colours, sir,' Summers had reminded Turk at dusk. 'Shall we stop for colours?' He had torn the knee of his trousers and his palms were blistered. Turk frowned. 'What for? This isn't bloody Spithead. Just pull the damn thing down.' When the last box had been stowed and the magazine hatch slammed shut, he picked up his jacket and glanced around at the fatigued hands. 'That'll do. Secure. Tomorrow morning we'll go across to Dunoon and swing the compass. That'll put us a day ahead of our programme, so I intend to carry out speed trials down to Lamlash, on Arran, where there'll be a make-and-mend for both watches. There's some good draught Younger's in Lamlash, no naval patrols, and mobs of Glasgow girls on holiday, all waiting for a chance to be ravished before they go home. The First Lieutenant will issue condoms to all men who want them, so if you clew up with a nap hand it'll be your own fault — and you'll be off this ship faster than a dose of Eno's.'

*

The weather had warmed. Lamlash was splashed with sunshine and, if there were hardly mobs of Glasgow shopgirls anxious to be ravished, there were certainly gratifying numbers, mildly bored with a resort that offered little recreation other than bracing walks and fine views of passing ships, who were willing to have a liaison with a shore-strolling sailor. There was first, however, a well-defined verbal ritual to be followed — a mutual probing of potential — that could no more be neglected than the mating gyrations of a pair of guinea-fowl. It was during this preliminary exchange that the girl, who assumed an air of distant disdain and the sailor one of devil-may-care, attempted to establish the degree of familiarity the partnership would reach. Once this phase of banter and innuendo had been entered into, it was difficult for either to withdraw with dignity.

It was important that the girl should not fraternize too readily; a fiction of reluctant virginity must be maintained. Over-eagerness could generate a wariness in the predator, and this was not conducive to the conclusion that both had determined upon. Lobby Ludd was therefore alarmed when, somewhat early in the proceedings, Jennie MacGillis announced 'Och, I ken what ye mean, but ma hole's too wee.'

Even Walt and Perk were momentarily disconcerted, and eyed their own consorts guardedly. All the tactical rules had suddenly been flouted. 'Is that a fact?' Lobby Ludd enquired. They had reached, by invitation, the Cuddy Nook, a grassy, enshrubbed venue obviously favoured by amatory couples because the grass was comfortably flattened in the more obscure places. 'Yer'd never believe it,' Perk said gallantly, 'if yer didn't know.'

The young ladies from Pollokshields were unabashed. 'She's having ye on,' scoffed Maggie Fraser. 'Wasn't she only sayin', the other nicht, that the black American she picked up in Union Street was rigged like a bluidy stallion, an' it was marvellous?'

'Like a bluidy steam-pump,' Jessie Duncan nodded.

'Is that a fact?' Lobby Ludd asked again, unable immediately to think of anything more relevant. His sexual appetite was less sharp than it had been earlier.

'Aye,' Jennie MacGillis recalled nostalgically. 'A big black bunk-up machine. Smashin'.' Lobby Ludd glanced at Perk, and Perk glanced at Walt. None had much regard for the finer points of courtship, but there were bleedin' limits.

'Well — ' Lobby Ludd chuckled, and looked at his watch. Jennie MacGillis, aggressively chewing, plucked an elastic tendril of gum from between her lips, regarded it critically over the tip of her nose, and then replaced it. 'Ye've no got a dose, have ye? It was a bluidy sailor last time, an' I was goin' ta the clinic for weeks.' Perk began to whistle tunelessly, and then Maggie Fraser said, 'Are we gang to stand aroon here like spare pricks at a weddin', then? Do ye want a grind, or dinna ye?' Lobby Ludd was relieved that the question had been directed at Perk, and not at himself, and Walt was saying nothing.

'As a matter o' fact' — Perk frowned, then looked at his own watch — 'there ain't a lot o' time, see — '

'Time?' Jennie MacGillis echoed. 'How much time do ye want? Do ye think ye're gang to leave it in soak a' bluidy nicht?'

'Well,' Perk explained, 'there's the preliminaries, an' it takes a bit ter work up ter full revs, see.' He appealed to Lobby Ludd. 'You're the bleedin' killick, mate. You're supposed ter be in charge.'

'There's plenty o' time,' Lobby Ludd decided. 'There's time fer six grinds. Only let's 'ave a bit o 'finesse, see. If the parties will jes' find a place that's a bit private, an' then sing out when they're ready — ?'

'Ye're bluidy fussy, aren't ye?' Maggie Fraser retorted. 'If ye ha' a bucket o' sand, I'll sing ye the Desert Song.'

'There's some things that's sacred,' Lobby Ludd said.

'Och, Maggie,' Jennie MacGillis snorted, 'come awa' and get yer knicks doon. I dinna walk a' this bluidy way for nothin' — an' we ha' ta be back in Glasga' tomorrow.'

'Ye'd think,' Jessie Duncan sniffed, 'that they was doin' us a bluidy favour.' Several moments later she glared at Walt from behind a tangle of furze. 'D'ye want ma fist? I'm no sittin' here long in ma bare arrse — '

'In case yer ain't soddin' guessed,' Loddy Ludd told Perk and Walt, 'we are goin' ter take independent avoiding action.'

'At a bleedin' rate o' knots,' Perk agreed. They ran for the road, followed by shrill expletives.

'Shave off,' Walt panted. 'We'll never know what we missed.'

*

The dull Home Fleet grey with which LCF49 had been painted was now replaced by convoluting white and blue, calculated to persuade the enemy that the ship was something different, or was not there at all. In her speed trials, with her diesel motors delivering 920 brake horse power, she had achieved eleven knots. Emergency full speed, during which her funnel vomited a massive cloud of black smoke, added another knot, but the vibration in the after mess-deck was so violent that every breakable artefact had been broken, and locker doors burst open to spill their contents on to a deck already carpeted with sugar, tea, pickles and milk. The galley chimney had collapsed in a welter of soot, and the latrine on which Able Seaman Perkins had been sitting regurgitated its contents explosively, to his bitter indignation.

It was the autumn of 1943, and the shipyards of the Clyde, Tyne, Mersey, Thames and Lagan were launching hundreds of new vessels and converting scores of others — large ships to carry smaller ones, small ships to carry men, tanks and guns, ships to beach, to fight or bombard, to take wounded, to control communications or direct aircraft, to repair damage, cook food or lay pipelines, or merely be sunk inshore to provide weather protection for others. Of every conceivable shape and purpose, some sleek and powerful, others ungainly and slow, they were gathering in flotillas, training, experimenting, often improvising, but always growing in experience and confidence. Progressively they would be moving southward to the harbours and rivers of the Channel coast, where the vast invasion armada was slowly assembling — Forces G, J, O, S, and U, principally British — in preparation for one momentous event, the landing of an Anglo-American army on the fortified shore of occupied France. That event would take place on a yet unspecified D-Day, at a yet unknown H-Hour.

Successful landings had been achieved in the Mediterranean and the Pacific earlier in the year, but none had been on the massive scale necessary to beach the Atlantic Wall, and there was speculation on the fortifications that had to be stormed — sixteen inch gun emplacements, minefields, concrete bunkers bristling with machine-guns, wire, underwater 'dragons' teeth', mortars and flame-throwers — and these were only the weapons that the enemy had allowed to be news-filmed. There would be others, still secret, as diabolically efficient as only the Germans could invent.

The other side of the Channel was an unknown that, one day, had to be faced. Men joked about it occasionally but there was seldom any serious discussion. The prospect was still remote and, if one did not think about it, well, it might go away. Combined Operations, the navy's assault command, was still something of a joke among the battleships, cruisers and carriers of general service; very many of its personnel were serving in their first ships, and the few regular naval men drafted resentfully into the command were vociferously critical. Shipboard conditions were not good, and crew amenities were minimal. Designers had wasted no refinements in ships that would probably be redundant after only one landing operation, and overlooked the fact that crews might well be living aboard for ten to twelve months prior to it. Except when on passage, it had been assumed, facilities such as canteens, baths, laundries, cooking, refrigeration, off-duty sleep and recreation would be provided by parent ships. In the event, however, parent ships were never provided.

The seamen's after mess-deck in major landing craft, immediately abaft the engine-room, with the propeller shafts underfoot and the exposed steering shaft just above head height, was so noisy and fiercely vibratory as to be almost intolerable. It was difficult to converse without shouting, to eat without spilling, impossible to write or sew, and a newcomer would consider sleep inconceivable under such circumstances — but in fact men did sleep.

The vessels were flat-bottomed and of shallow draught, so that, despite twin rudders and screws, they were difficult to manoeuvre and, unless heavily handled, were prone to ignore the wheel; leeway was best applied in multiples of twenty-five degrees. In only a moderate swell they rolled alarmingly.

Navigation was by dead reckoning and, as the craft responded markedly to wind and current, open-sea passages presented problems and inshore navigation in darkness or bad visibility could be hazardous. In addition to flags and signal lamps, a Marconi TV5 transmitter-receiver allowed radio communication on local port waves, and portable VHF equipment was installed for specific operations. The only codebook carried was the simple, direct-conversion Fleet Code, changed monthly.

*

A company of sixty Royal Marines embarked at Troon, led by Lieutenants Bunter and Taplow, two sergeants and several corporals. They had made a tiring journey from Portsmouth unaware that, within two days, LCF49 would be sailing for Southampton. They were all landsmen. 'Yer can always tell,' Walt said, watching the new arrivals descend to their mess-deck, forward. 'They go down ladders backwards, like parties. They'll start being seasick any bleedin' minute.'

Lieutenant Bunter was large and ruddy, with an impressive moustache and a hearty manner that promised to be tiresome. His shorter colleague, Taplow, was similarly moustached but less hearty, probably because he was the junior. Both were immaculately tailored and carried short, leather-covered sticks for no apparent purpose other than to slap their thighs and point at things.

'Good morning, sir,' Bunter said briskly, saluting Turk. 'We're delighted to be aboard.' Taplow also saluted. 'Delighted to be aboard, sir,' he confirmed. Both shot quick glances at Turk's tartan carpet-slippers.

'Would you care to inspect the men, sir?' Bunter enquired.

Turk frowned, 'Why? What have they got?' He turned as a sergeant began to scream orders at men carrying their bags across the gangplank. 'Tell that clown to bloody well pipe down, will you? Those rifles and bayonets can be stowed. I doubt if we'll ever need to make a bayonet charge. And be careful with those sticks. You'll poke someone's eye out.'

'What about ceremonials, sir? Won't you want a daily colour guard? Actually, we're not entitled to a bugler, but we've got one — '

'This isn't the bloody Rodney,' Sub-Lieutenant Summers grunted, and Turk smothered a grin. Summers was noticeably less spruce than he had been a week earlier. There was a mended tear in one leg of his trousers, his shoes were beginning to scuff, and there was a smear of blue paint on the peak of his cap. 'And if your chap starts blowing a bloody bugle in the morning, he's likely to get it wrapped around his head.' He sniffed belligerently.

'Ah — yes, well — ' Bunter chuckled, and smoothed his moustache. Taplow also chuckled.

'This afternoon,' Turk ordered, 'all guns will be stripped and cleaned under the direction of the OA, and magazines loaded. Tomorrow you're going to be shooting at a target towed by aircraft, off Ardrossan.'

'Good show,' Bunter nodded, and laughed at Taplow. 'I don't think that'll give us much trouble, eh, Taps? Our bunch is pretty good, y'know.'

Taplow nodded and laughed. 'Pretty good.'

'Only this time,' Turk advised, 'you'll be moving at ten knots and going up and down at the same time. The target will also be travelling at about a hundred and twenty miles an hour.'

'*Per Mare, per Terrain*, sir. Just let the dog see the rabbit. What do you say, Taps?' Taplow agreed. 'Absolutely. No trouble.'

Perk and Walt had found their steel helmets. 'It ain't that I'm nervous,' Walt said, 'but what goes up must bleedin' come down.'

The aircraft, a slow-flying Anson, approached from the eastward, circled speculatively, then began to reel out a target drogue on several hundred feet of tow-line. *'Ready when you are,'* flashed its lamp. *'First run from astern.'*

The LCF's guns opened fire simultaneously with a deafening roar. The galley chimney collapsed in a frenzy of soot that swirled over the bridge, blinding everyone, and the deck shuddered. The ERA, watching events with head and shoulders protruding from the engine-room hatch, bit through the stem of his pipe, fell off the ladder and sprained an ankle, and SBA Peach, with eyes clenched, ran into the wheelhouse, not observing that the steel door was shut. His nose bled.

Lieutenant Bunter shouted excitedly. 'Ceasefire! Cease fire!' He pointed. 'It's a hit, sir — first time! Well done, chaps!' Lieutenant Taplow shouted, 'Well done, chaps!' The distant drogue, tangling, was falling into the sea, but the aircraft had banked steeply and its signal lamp was blinking madly.

'Please fire at target, not at me. Tow line has been cut six feet behind my tail.'

'Obviously a stray shot,' Bunter decided. 'Probably a defective round. If we picked up that drogue, we'd find it was riddled.' Turk wiped soot from his face and grunted doubtfully.

The Anson was reeling out a second target and now began a run from ahead. *'Please remember,'* the lamp flashed, *'the target is the one with no wings'.*

Lieutenant Bunter snorted. 'I shouldn't be surprised if he hasn't been reduced to target-towing because his nerves have cracked.' Taplow snorted agreement.

The guns hammered again. Towing the drogue, the aircraft flew the second run down the port side, the third up the starboard side, and the fourth from beam to beam. 'It's incredible how that target stays in one piece,' Bunter puzzled. 'You'd think it would be in shreds.'

'In rags,' Taplow nodded.

'No hits observed,' the Anson reported. *'I will come closer. Easier for you, safer for me.'*

'Bloody cheek,' Bunter retorted. 'He's a lousy pilot, anyway. He's never flown straight for more than five seconds at a time.'

The aircraft made two more runs, then commented, *'No hits seen on target but observer reports tail wheel shot away. Am returning to base for stiff brandy.'*

'It's a damn good job he wasn't carrying bombs,' Turk said, 'or he might have tried to fight back.'

'I don't understand it,' Bunter complained. 'It must be the gun-sights. Does the ordnance artificer know what he's doing?'

'It must be the gun-sights,' Taplow nodded.

'The OA checked all calibrations yesterday,' Turk sighed, 'and he did his apprenticeship with Vickers, where they make the bloody things.'

Lobby Ludd turned from the twelve-inch lamp. 'Signal from the coastguard station, sir. "Ardrossan police report numerous complaints of damage to roofs, windows and glasshouses from falling missiles. Are you responsible?"'

'If it wasn't the aircraft disintegrating,' Turk mused, 'it must have been us.' He frowned. 'On second thoughts, Bunter, perhaps your Marines should keep their bayonets. They might be our only bloody hope.'

*

'Someone oughter tell Churchill,' Perk said on the mess-deck, when LCF49 had regained Troon. 'We oughter surrender now, before it's too bleedin' late.' He looked into the mirror. 'I can't decide if my 'air will go white before it all falls out. It's going ter be touch an' go.' ERA Gilbert, who had a last-chance assignation ashore with a cinema usherette, was trying to borrow a size twelve right shoe to accommodate his sprained ankle, and SBA Peach had taken sal volatile. Stoker Bowles had size twelves, but wanted to know if he was expected to hop around on one bleedin' foot while ERA Gilbert was breaking a bit off behind the Roxy.

'Number One,' Lieutenant Turk ordered, 'shore leave will terminate at midnight. The ship is under sailing orders and we slip at oh-eight-double-oh, for Southampton. The first leg is the longest — to Appledore in North Devon — and you and I will be watch and watch about. After Appledore we'll call at Falmouth, Dartmouth, Portland, and then the Solent. Lieutenants Bunter and Taplow will therefore be responsible for all other routine duties.' He considered. 'Bunter can start by inspecting libertymen, doing rounds, and checking that all men are aboard at midnight. Taplow will be Officer of the Day tomorrow. As almost all the naval personnel are sea dutymen, I don't want their mess-deck treated like one of your Eastney barrackrooms. Leave them alone as much as possible. All hands will be shaken at oh-six-three-oh.'

'Ah, yes,' Bunter said. 'Heave ho, heave ho, lash up and stow.'

'No, I shouldn't if I were you,' Turk advised. 'Leave it to the coxswain. You might hear some bad language.'

On the fore-deck Lieutenant Bunter, with stick under arm, inspected two ranks of rigid Royal Marine libertymen with scrupulous care, then turned to the handful of less rigid sailors. The lieutenant was unfamiliar with the niceties of naval uniform, but he moved from man to man, eyeing each, nodding approval. He did not nod when he reached ERA Gilbert.

'There is no doubt,' he frowned, 'that you have one foot considerably longer than the other.'

Surprised, Gilbert looked at his feet and then up at Lieutenant Bunter. 'That's right, sir. I thought you'd been told. It's an occupational hazard, on account of always having one foot on the baffle compressor in the reciprocating evaporator, and the other on the combustion utilizer sprocket — very common among engine-room artificers. There was an article about it in the Steam and Diesel Engineer, with a graph.'

Bunter hesitated, uncertain, but Gilbert's face was innocently earnest. 'Ah, yes,' Bunter agreed. 'I think I remember.' He withdrew one pace smartly and smoothed his moustache. 'Very good. Carry on, libertymen.'

*

The Indian summer of 1943 was fading into autumn as LCF49 pushed her ungainly hull through a calm Irish Sea. Sometimes, to eastward, there would be a green-fringed coastline, of Galloway, the Isle of Man, Anglesey, Pembroke, and sometimes only an unbroken horizon of sea. The quiet night skies were crowded with stars, the ship darkened except for minimum navigation lights, and it was a time for thinking. The war seemed distant and the ship no part of it. The Allies had overrun Sicily and landed in Italy, but progress was slow. The Russians had recovered Smolensk, and the tide had turned against the Japanese in the Pacific, but these events seemed peripheral, almost irrelevant. A final conclusion would only be achieved by a massive assault on the German fortress of Western Europe, a prospect that, as yet, baffled the imagination. It did not seem possible to the largely inexperienced crews of hundreds of craft like LCF49 that, sooner or later, they were going to be thrown against the armour of the enemy's Channel defences. It had been suggested that the French and Belgian coasts were held only by second-rate reserve troops, but they had heard these stories before — that the Germans had wooden tanks, had clothing made from paper, lacked food, oil and steel, that the Japanese were shortsighted, were untrained in jungle fighting, had obsolete weapons and, because of a rice diet, lacked stamina. None of these shortcomings seemed to have made much difference when the chips were down.

*

During the second night on passage, some forty miles westwards of Lundy Island, the tired voice of the telegraphist came from the wheelhouse voice-pipe.

'W/T to bridge. From Milford Haven, sir. Red Severn.'

At the bridge rail Sub-Lieutenant Summers, who had been lost in reverie, whirled guiltily, grappling for comprehension. 'Red seven? What's that, Ludd? Alter course seventy degrees to starboard? Or is it port — ?'

'No, sir,' Lobby Ludd explained. 'Red Severn. It's a broadcast to all ships keeping watch on port wave, not just us, meaning Air Raid Warning Red over the Severn area. But we don't have to — ' There was no urgency yet. A single unidentified aircraft or a lone enemy intruder somewhere over southwest England was no immediate concern of a ship at sea in darkness. In a few more moments, almost certainly, the same wireless station would transmit 'White Severn,' indicating that the warning was cancelled.

'Air raid?' Sub-Lieutenant Summers flung himself at the action alarm, and an explosive, ear-splitting hammer of bells flooded the silent ship from end to end, penetrating every deck, every compartment. 'No, sir!' Lobby Ludd protested, flinching. 'There ain't no need!' But it was too late. There were muffled shouts from below, the clatter of feet on steel decks, the clang of watertight doors. The magazine hatch crashed open and men were stumbling from ladders, dragging on clothing, trailing helmets, cursing in the darkness, and already the first boxes of ammunition were being hoisted to the foredeck. Lieutenant Bunter was bawling, 'Load, load, load!'

'W/T to bridge. From Milford Haven, sir. White Severn.'

'Red warning cancelled, sir,' Lobby Ludd said.

Lieutenant Turk had reached the bridge, struggling into a duffel coat. 'What's the score, Number One?' Behind him Bunter and Taplow were climbing the ladder and, in anticipation, the galley chimney had been lowered. The ship's naval crewmen in wheel-house and engine-room had already reported closed up and ready for action, and an apprehensive SBA Peach had appeared with a haversack of splints and dressings.

'Ah — I think I may have been a little premature, sir,' Summers explained. 'There was a Red warning — '

Turk drew a deep breath. 'You mean you turned out the entire bloody ship at three in the morning for an area alert?' Lobby Ludd polished the glass of the twelve-inch lamp with his cuff.

Lieutenant Bunter, steel-helmeted, hung with gasmask, Webley .38, life-belt, binoculars and whistle, saluted grimly. 'All guns loaded and ready, sir.'

Turk looked at his watch. 'It took you ninety-five seconds, Bunter, and that's not bloody good enough. We could have been blown to pieces by the time you got yourself rigged up like a blasted Christmas-tree. We're going to have a lot more of these exercise alarms until you've got your time down to below fifty seconds, so you and your men are going to take your fingers out — or you're not going to get much sleep.' He nodded. 'All right. Secure and stand down.'

Bunter's jaw dropped. 'Exercise, sir?' He swallowed. 'Don't you think that the officers ought to know in advance? I mean, exercises without warning are a good thing for the men, sir, but for officers — ' His voice trailed. Turk's scowl froze further debate. Bunter saluted again and retired with Taplow at his heels.

Sub-Lieutenant Summers shot a glance at Lobby Ludd, still applying himself to the twelve-inch lamp. 'I'm sorry, sir. I seem to have made a cock-up.'

Turk chuckled. 'Don't apologize, Sub. According to the book you were probably right. When I did my first fortnight at sea, in Ramillies, I thought I saw a ghost, one night, on the quarterdeck. I was nineteen. I threw a paraffin-lamp at it, and it caught the deck on fire. Afterwards, the ghost turned out to be the Rear-Admiral, in his nightshirt, spewing over the after rail. Next day, nobody talked about it, but I believe there's still a scorch-mark on Ramillies' quarterdeck where the lamp exploded.' He chuckled again, then shrugged. 'I'd rather have fifty false alarms than ignore one genuine hazard. But don't tell Bunter.' He walked to the screen and leaned on his elbows. 'I hope it's a nice day tomorrow. I understand he's taking the Marines for a route march.'

Three

It was a very nice day in Appledore, cloudless and warm. The Royal Marines, in field order, each with corned beef sandwiches and an apple, and led by Lieutenants Bunter and Taplow, tramped off determinedly into the Devon hinterland. The sailors, released on watchkeepers' leave soon after midday, drank beer until closing time, then stimulated the proceedings of a local fete, where they listened to the band, ogled the girls, played quoits, guessed unsuccessfully at the weight of a pig, and participated noisily in the sack race. Perk won a small goldfish in a glass bowl, the second prize in the knobbly knees competition.

At the approach of the evening licensing hour they abandoned frivolity but remained in the Chequers only briefly, leaving a large and irate farmer locked in fierce dispute with the proprietor because he had found a small goldfish swimming in his cider. After more beer, ice cream and fish and chips, SBA Peach was sick in the refuse bin at the bus stop, while his fellows sympathetically pounded him between his shoulder blades. Walt tore his collar on a barbed wire fence while urinating in privacy. ERA Gilbert suddenly discovered that he had lost his right shoe, which belonged to Stoker Bowles, and on return to the ship fell down the mess-deck hatch and sprained his left ankle. Everyone agreed that it had been a bleedin' marvellous run ashore.

Southampton, when they got there — Perk said if they got there and he didn't soddin' believe it — would bring Lobby Ludd nearer to London than he had ever been during his naval career, a circumstance of debatable advantage. It was not that he entertained any ill-feeling towards London specifically. Indeed, he was a loyal native of the metropolis, and his mother maintained a modest sweetshop in Walham Green. Lobby Ludd was fond of his widowed mother, although not extravagantly devoted to her. She was one of those simple, happy people to whom any event beyond their immediate vicinity was of no consequence and probably incomprehensible. The war concerned her only in terms of rations, the black-out, and the difficulty of obtaining an elastic stocking for her varicose veins. Of greater moment to Lobby Ludd was the narrowing proximity of Freda Harris.

The trouble with becoming closely acquainted with a party, Lobby Ludd explained to Perk and Walt, was that as soon as you screwed her a few times she began talking about getting spliced. Women didn't seem to understand that there was such a thing as platonic sexual intercourse with no ulterior motives. Being introduced to her parents was the red light, and when her father was the Reverend Harris of St Barnabas's Church, and asked you to instruct the Scouts in knots and flag-wagging that was the time to volunteer for a foreign draft chit.

Freda Harris was determined to be led to the altar, despite the hostility he had provoked in her parents. No, that was not entirely true. The Reverend Harris still believed that he, Lobby Ludd, had been reciting Kipling's ballads to the Scouts in the church hall although, to be bleedin' honest, he had delivered 'Eskimo Nell' and then 'Alice Brewer', which rhymed with 'screw her' and proceeded to describe exactly how. Mrs Harris, however, had suffered no such blissful illusions, and Lobby Ludd's protest that, delicately, he had substituted Alice Brewer for Alice Tucker did nothing to change her view that he was drunken and licentious soldiery.

'It's only Mother,' Freda Harris had consoled him at Paddington Station. 'She can never forget that she once met the Prince of Wales at a sale of work in Thornton Heath, and she was absolutely livid about Mrs Simpson. Of course, if I had an engagement ring — ' Lobby Ludd had glanced gratefully at the station clock, which indicated that there remained no time in which to seek a jeweller. 'I'll send you my finger size,' she promised. 'A solitaire. Anyway, I'll be twenty-one next year. I mean, we can't go on like this, can we? I know you're always careful, but just suppose. You'd only have to forget once and I'll be at the pre-natal clinic in flat shoes getting orange-juice coupons — '

'So she sent me this card with an 'ole in it,' Lobby Ludd told Perk and Walt, and showed them. 'It ain't that I mind buying a ring, it's the ramifications.'

Neither Perk nor Walt knew what ramifications were, but agreed that it was a bleedin' liberty.

'Once yer buy a ring,' Perk said, 'she can sue yer fer contempt o' court. Yer could be payin' maintenance fer bleedin' years.' There had been something in the paper about Errol Flynn. 'He's still payin' thousands o' pounds fer a nibble he 'ad before the war, mate. It's diabolical. Nobody believes a bloke when he sez he was talked into it.'

*

The weather was becoming less kind as the ship rounded Land's End into long, grey Atlantic rollers crested with white. The shallow hull rose and fell, with the square bows smashing into the sea and exploding spray; the halyards hummed in the wind like harp-strings and the smoke from the swaying funnel was torn away into a threatening sky. Oil-skinned Royal Marines huddled miserably at their gun-stations, white-faced as the deck heeled sickeningly. Few had touched their breakfast; the very thought of food was anathema, and death had lost its sting. The bathroom, swilling in several inches of filthy water, reeked of vomit.

On the bridge Lieutenant Turk, in muffler and carpet-slippers, showed no sign of concern. The ship's behaviour was uncomfortable, but it was entirely predictable and not yet hazardous. He had navigated smaller vessels through considerably worse, and instinct would tell him immediately the moment had arrived to think about storm-evasion measures. That moment was not yet. For the present it was all good experience for the queasy stomachs on the foredeck.

Sub-Lieutenant Summers, to his relief and delight, was equally unaffected, and even more delighted to observe that Bunter and Taplow were suffering all the horrors of sea-sickness while trying to pretend they were not. In the ill-ventilated wardroom both had declined breakfast and mid-forenoon coffee. Taplow seemed unwilling to be long separated from the hand basin in his cabin, and for two hours Bunter had been studying, with dull eyes, a small-arms manual without progressing beyond the second page. He raised a bleak face at Summers's jaunty entrance, shuddered, but forced a teeth-clenched smile. Summers rubbed his hands briskly, then balanced himself carefully as he poured himself a gin. 'Can I pour you chaps a snort?' he asked. 'The sun's over the yardarm.'

Taplow looked away. Bunter, by an incredible effort, forced a laugh. 'Ha, ha.' There was a white ring around his lips. 'I suppose', he said casually, 'that the captain will be running for Penzance?'

'Penzance?' Summers's eyes widened. 'Whatever for? It's a bit untidy, but nothing much. It'll be worse off the Lizard. I shouldn't be surprised if we don't start shipping it green. That'll have a few of your chaps emptying their guts over the side.' He chuckled.

Taplow swallowed. 'I've just remembered,' he gritted, 'I have to supervise the rum issue.' He rose, then thought about rum, and his eyes glazed. He stumbled for his cabin.

'He looks a bit frayed around the edges,' Summers observed as the wardroom lurched. 'That reminds me. Have you inspected the heads this morning? They smell like an explosion in a cess-pit. The trouble is that the sea pressure at the outlet forces the stuff back up the pipe, and it all spills over.'

Bunter stared at page two. Someone had once told him that, to fight off nausea, one should think happy thoughts, but the mental picture of overspilling latrines refused to go away. Vickers Machine Gun,.303 inch. Weight thirty pounds without water, forty pounds with water — water.

'We haven't got anyone who knows much about plumbing,' Summers went on remorselessly. 'I suppose Gilbert, the ERA — '

Bunter clutched desperately at the change of subject. 'Ah, yes. You know, it's quite incredible about Gilbert's feet. Actually, I could have sworn it was his right foot, but when I saw him yesterday it was his left.' He frowned. 'I could have sworn it was his right. Anyway, I suppose he'll get some sort of disability pension?'

Summers pondered. 'Disability pension? Gilbert? What for?'

'It's this business of the baffle compressor and the utiliser sprocket. You probably read the article in the Steam and Diesel Engineer. I mean, dammit, it's almost obscene. You'd think there'd be some sort of manipulative treatment. It's not my business, but it could never happen in the Marines. What sort of future is there for a man like that? With all the resources of modem science, something should have been done at the first sign, instead of letting the man become a freak. Why hasn't he been invalided out? I don't understand it.'

Nor did Summers. He did not recall seeing ERA Gilbert enjoying anything but rude health, and he had never appeared disturbed about a freakish future, or by anything. Indeed, the enduring insouciance of men like Gilbert, Perkins, Walters and Ludd was a quality of which he was reluctantly envious. It must be Lieutenant Bunter. Perhaps sea-sickness, like too much sun, generated hallucinations.

'Oh, that,' he nodded, and decided to have a second gin. He would have another look at ERA Gilbert; he might have missed something. 'You ought to have the afternoon in your bunk — after lunch. If you think you're going to spew up, it's best to have something in your stomach.'

The steward peered from the pantry. 'Did you say lunch, sir? Will you 'ave it now?'

'Good idea,' Summers decided. 'For two, please. What are we on?'

'Savoury brown soup, sir. Pilchard-and-potato casserole au gratin and green pea puree. Then suet pudding with lemon curd.'

'Fine.' Summers glanced over his shoulder as Bunter's cabin door slammed. 'But on second thoughts you'd better make it just one.'

*

Summers climbed to the bridge at 1230 to relieve Turk. The wind had risen appreciably, tearing off the crests of the rollers as the ship crashed into them and enveloping the bows in vicious spray. To port the coastline was lost to view, hidden by a haze of grey vapour. Turk's oilskins streamed, his cap was sodden.

'Why has "Up Spirits" only just been piped, Number One?' he asked. 'What's Taplow doing?'

Summers grimaced. 'Sorry, sir. I had to do it myself. He couldn't face the smell.' With a few more days of weather like this, he calculated, his cap badge would be as nicely tarnished as Turk's. 'I think they were both hoping that you would put into Penzance.'

'Penzance?' The other laughed. 'We're not even putting into Falmouth. With this bloody sea running I want to keep well clear of the Lizard, so we may as well push on to Dartmouth. It's only another eighty miles — so long as our bows hold together — and better than several hours of beam sea, which could be nasty for the cook.'

'Before you go, sir,' Summers said, hesitating, 'I suppose you haven't noticed anything odd about Gilbert, the ERA, have you? A disability?'

'Gilbert?' Turk stared. 'A disability? No, I haven't. A disability? What sort of disability?'

'Well, it's all a bit vague, sir. I think it might be a club foot, but I'm not sure which one. In fact I'm not even sure — '

'A club foot? Good God!'

'If he hasn't, sir, I think we ought to keep an eye on Bunter — '

'Bunter? Why? What's he got? A hunch back?'

'Ah, no sir. But he could be a little fruit-cakey — purely temporarily, of course. I mean, that's if Gilbert hasn't got a club foot, or whatever it is.'

Turk wiped salt water from his face and drew a deep breath. 'You haven't been hitting the bottle, have you, Number One? If you take my advice you'll leave it alone if you're coming on watch. Course one-oh-five, ten knots, until sixteen hundred. We'll talk about the other thing when you're sober.'

*

A dozen or more Combined Operations vessels were moored, midstream, in the Dart estuary — tank and infantry landing craft — whose crews eyed the arrival of the newcomer with brief interest. It was mildly comforting to be only one of a number of ugly ducklings, and a blissful relief to most of LCF49's crew to see firm land and rooftops. A wan-faced Lieutenant Taplow and a detachment of Royal Marines stood to attention on the fore-deck as the ship entered harbour, and Sub-Lieutenant Summers, forward, stood by to pick up the buoy. Summers, within the space of three weeks, had become very raffish. He swaggered. His cap badge was fashionably dull, and he wore the mended tear in the knee of his trousers like a decoration for valour. He had taken great care to shave badly each morning, and he intended to buy himself a pair of carpet-slippers in Dartmouth.

Within minutes of securing, a trot-boat manned by Wrens was alongside with mail and a signal by hand from NOIC, joined subsequently by a NAAFI drifter with canteen supplies. The Wrens were a novelty not to be ignored, but they were more than a match for the speculative sailors and parried all overtures with practised verbal wit. 'It ain't no good,' complained Walt, defeated. 'They've all got padlocks on their pants instead of elastic.'

'Ah, Gilbert,' the First Lieutenant said, keeping his gaze away from the other's feet. 'Er — are you quite all right? I mean — feeling fit and all that?'

'In the pink, sir,' the ERA responded, surprised. 'I did 'ave dhobey-itch, but Peach gave me some stuff. And yourself, sir? Quite well, I'ope?'

'Oh — yes — quite well,' Summers went forward to look at the moorings.

'Ah — Gilbert — ' Lieutenant Turk had paused at the foot of the bridge ladder. 'Gilbert — '; He lowered his voice. 'Confidentially, I was just wondering. Is there something you feel you'd like to tell me about?'

Gilbert considered. 'Well, sir, diesel fuel's down to about fifty per cent, and the clutch bearing on number two runs a bit hot at maximum revs, but it's nothing ter bust a gut over — '

'No, I mean about yourself. Any physical difficulties? Anything medical?'

Gilbert was mildly embarrassed. 'I did tell the First Lieutenant, sir. It wasn't nothing much, and the SBA painted some blue stuff on — '

'On your foot?' Turk whispered.

'No, sir.' The ERA'S face was a blank. He glanced around and then leaned forward conspiratorially. 'On my testicals.'

*

As LCF49 moved eastward along the Channel coast the build-up of an invasion fleet was becoming daily more evident. Flotillas of landing craft were exercising in Lyme Bay, on Portland's Chesil Beach, and emerging from Poole Harbour. The creeks of the Isle of Wight, the Solent, Southampton Water and the Hamble all harboured clustered lines of assault vessels, and shore maintenance bases had mushroomed — HMS *Squid* in Southampton, *Turtle* in Poole, *Vectis* in Cowes — within the Portsmouth command in which was also situated Combined Operations HQ, Fort Southwick. The docks and yards of Southampton, abandoned by the big passenger lines of the transatlantic trade, were beginning to congest with dozens of smaller, oddly shaped ships, whose role it was sometimes difficult to guess and unwise to enquire into. Quite suddenly the designation 'Second Front', for so long a distant, nebulous thing, was assuming a new meaning. It really was going to happen.

To emphasize it, all craft of the British Force 'J' assault fleet, concentrating on Southampton and Cowes were ordered to paint a broad, distinguishing red stripe around funnel and bridge. Force 'G', out of Weymouth, bore a wide green stripe, and Force 'S', operating from Portsmouth and Newhaven, a blue stripe. Nobody in the amphibious armada, however, had yet heard of Operation Overlord, or assault phase Neptune. There was no whisper, yet, of beachheads Gold, Juno and

Sword, or Omaha and Utah. Whether the assault, when it happened, would be launched against the coast of Normandy, of Holland and Belgium or the Cotentin Peninsula, the Pas de Calais or even Brittany, was a question that defied speculation. On balance, it hardly seemed to matter.

In the Old Docks of Southampton LCF49 was joined by four more LCFs and two LCGs, an ugly little brood of ships that, collectively, mustered four 4.7-inch and four four-inch ex-destroyer guns, sixteen two-pounder 'pom-poms' and sixty-three 20-mm Oerlikons — a formidable armament capable of remaining afloat within yards of a beach or, if necessary, being run ashore through the surf. The flotilla, tied low against jetties that had been built for the ocean giants of Cunard and Union Castle, eyed each other warily and were gazed at by the puzzled eyes of dockyard workers. Six months before, in distant Washington, the Anglo-American High Command had decided that the cross-Channel invasion would be mounted in early May 1944. That left only the short winter intervening, and there was much to be done.

The ships' crews were raw yet, but growing less so as the weeks passed — those weeks of exercising in bitter weather between Portland Bill to westward and Beachy Head to the east, manoeuvring by flags, by light, gunnery shoots with air-towed and surface targets, or against the cliffs of the Isle of Wight. There would be dark nights of groping off the Dorset coast, days of heaving green seas, of stinging sleet, of oaths and fingers blue with cold at the guns, wet clothes, eyes red-shot with fatigue. Not quickly, but surely, the Marines were losing their nausea and their landsmen's fumbling; they achieved their fifty seconds. Their nervous haste had gone and they were becoming a coordinated team, wasting neither time nor movement. Now, when the sodden drogues were dragged from the sea, they were ripped with shell-holes. The magazine hoist worked smoothly and the galley chimney no longer collapsed at the deck's first vibration. Lieutenants Bunter and Taplow learned a number of painful lessons, were better officers for it, and were still learning. Sub-Lieutenant Summers's carpet-slippers, with rabbits' ears, disintegrated quickly in the salt and grease of the after deck, and he reverted to leather halfboots.

'I reckon I was being considered fer a commission,' ERA Gilbert decided, 'until they found out about my dhobey-itch. Officers don't get dhobey-itch, only pruritis genitalia.'

Lobby Ludd was receiving ominous pink letters, postmarked Wimbledon Park, and Perk and Walt had invested in a Crown and Anchor Board.

*

The Reverend Harris had always experienced difficulty in distinguishing between his daughter's various swains, particularly when so many were in uniform and looked exactly alike. 'Are you the one that was shot down,' he asked 'or the one that sent Freda the nylon night-attire from America?' Lobby Ludd agreed that he had once been torpedoed, but had only brought a string bag of oranges from Gibraltar. 'Ah, yes,' Mr Harris nodded doubtfully. 'I remember. I only asked, my boy, because the night-attire must have been very expensive, and it's quite unwearable. To be frank, it's indecent.'

'It's disgusting,' Mrs Harris emphasized, being a devotee of shapeless flannelette to the ankle, calculated to unfailingly bridle male libido. She remembered Charlie Ludd very well. 'You always seem to come when we're going to the old people's whist,' she said, in that tone of voice that made it clear she knew exactly why.

Freda hastened to explain. 'We're going to browse through some lists,' she told them, without being more specific. 'And tomorrow we're going to Bravington's.' She frowned. 'Mother, have I still got my white prayer book? I think I've got everything else except something borrowed and something blue.' Savagely, Mrs Harris thrust home a hat pin, then fastened her bird-like eyes on Lobby Ludd. If looks could kill, he would have fallen, writhing. 'I think,' she pronounced, 'that you must have a long talk with the Reverend.' She paused to turn down the electric fire. 'Tonight. We shall try to get back early.'

'Not too early, I hope,' Freda giggled as the front door closed.

Lobby Ludd was pensive. 'What was all that about something borrowed an' something blue?'

'Charlie,' Freda said firmly, 'you've really got to start being serious. We can't keep performing on the sofa just on old people's whist nights. A girl wants security. Now, I've been reading about this scheme for servicemen who want to invest in a house after the war. It's called "A

Fireside for Your Family", and you pay something every month. I've sent for the forms. There was a picture of a lovely house with trees and a swimming-pool, but I expect that's extra. I was thinking of Walton-on-Thames; I've always liked that part — '

Lobby Ludd protested that he already allotted a pound a month to Bernard's so that he could have an occasional made-to-measure blue suit, but he didn't think Bernard's did houses.

'There you are, then,' Freda triumphed. 'That's a pound for a start.' On that reckoning, he pointed out, the war would have to last eighty years, even dispensing with a swimming-pool.

Freda pouted. 'You don't understand, Charlie. You'll just be paying instalments towards a deposit that will go towards the interest on a loan. Then, when you pay back the loan, there won't be so much interest.' It was all very simple.

Lobby Ludd lacked enthusiasm. For a start, Walton-on-Thames was a bit near Wimbledon and St Barnabas's Church, but, most of all, wasn't it just a little premature? 'It ain't me I'm thinking about,' he promised. 'I don't matter. It's you. Yer've 'ad a very sheltered life, and yer mustn't throw yerself away on the first 'andsome face yer meet. That's the trouble with wartime romances. And before yer know it, yer could be a widder.' He sighed. 'I'ate myself fer saying it, but we've jes' got ter wait. We can still'ave our fleeting moments — '

'On the old people's whist night,' she retorted. She went to the sideboard and extracted a bottle of the Reverend's homemade parsnip. 'Daddy made it in 1939. Nobody's drunk any since he trod on his glasses and did a pee in the broom-closet. We don't talk about it.' She poured a large glass and smiled at him.

Lobby Ludd smiled back. If she really thought that a glass of home-made jungle-juice was suddenly going to motivate any aspirations for a Fireside for His Family, then she was going to be brought up with a round turn. After the four-star paraffin that passed for brandy in La Linea, he could drink anything.

The home-made parsnip did nothing until it reached his gastric region, where it began to boil. Freda had disappeared. His eyes were turning to hot glue and everything was pink. He had the presence of mind to avoid breathing in the direction of the electric fire, but could do nothing about his rubber legs.

'Now, Charlie,' Freda said from the door. 'Just think. Wouldn't it be wonderful if every night was like this?' She regarded him solicitously. 'I did put a little whisky in it.'

She wore a dainty night-dress that reached only to her thighs, and she might have been wearing nothing; the nylon was almost transparent. 'It's American,' she told him, 'and it opens down the front, like this.' She demonstrated. 'And the label says "I Surrender".' Lubby Ludd's tongue seemed to be impossibly swollen, but he nodded

'I'm just trying to show you, Charlie,' she went on, curling up beside him and leaving her night-dress appealingly open, 'that there's more things in life than just squeezing my bumps in the back row of the Gaumont.'

Lobby Ludd agreed that he always thought there was; it was just a matter of time and opportunity, not to mention the home-made parsnip.

'Why,' Freda frowned, 'are sailors' trousers different to ordinary trousers?' He suggested that it wasn't so much that they were different but that she had his tapes entangled with a button of some consequence, although he was distressed to think that she recognized any disparity. Freda said that she did press her father's trousers when the bishop was expected.

'There,' she sighed. 'Don't pretend you don't like it, Charlie. I can tell. And it could be like this all the time, in front of our own fire. Just shut your eyes. I know exactly what's going to happen.'

'So do I,' snapped Mrs Harris, from behind them. 'And I've shut my eyes. If that naked fornicator isn't out of this house when I open them, I'll scream for the police ... '

Four

It was Christmas Day and, to the crew's disgust, LCF49 was duty ship for the twenty-four hours following noon. The men from the rest of the flotilla had gone ashore after a festive dinner of pork and stuffing, roast potatoes, sprouts, pudding and custard, and within minutes had scattered among the bars beyond the gate of the deserted dockyard. LCF49 had moved to an outer berth so that, if ordered to sea, there would be no delay in slipping her moorings.

The duty was one imposed in rotation on the craft of the flotilla, ensuring that at all times there was one vessel in Southhampton fully manned and prepared for leaving harbour at immediate notice. All hands were confined to the ship, and from midday a telegraphist maintained listening watch on Portsmouth's port wave, 2450 kc/s, by which medium emergency orders, if any, would be conveyed. The operator would not transmit unless directly called by Portsmouth, the control station, but would record all signals exchanged on the frequency, so that an early warning might be achieved of any developing situation that could demand the duty ship's participation. Such a demand had never been made during the flotilla's three months in Southampton. There had always been other ships, similarly moored in Portsmouth and Cowes, closer to the Channel, larger and faster than an eleven-knot assault craft, to deal with emergencies at sea. It would doubtless be the same today, and LCF49's vigil would be as abortive as it had always been before — only before it hadn't been soddin' Christmas Day.

Except for the unfortunate telegraphist, however, the afternoon was a make-and-mend — a period of no routine work. The seamen's mess-deck had been draped with bunting and, earlier, Lieutenant Turk had conceded that the rum ration should be issued neat instead of as grog, with water added. The officers had made their rounds, an occasion when formalities were relaxed, and there was considerable chaff. Sub-Lieutenant Summers, who had been attempting to cultivate a pugnacious beard but with only modest success, was greeted with a chorus of goat-like bleats which he accepted in good humour. Perk claimed that he had more hair on his right knee. The mess-tables were spread with the contents of parcels from home — cakes, fruit, a bowl of nuts — and Lieutenant Taplow dutifully sampled a slice of Stoker Bowles's black pudding, slightly damaged in the post.

The officers remained only briefly; there was a limit to camaraderie. They, too, would have preferred to be ashore, in the Polygon or the lounge of the Dolphin, but there would be drinks in the wardroom. The seamen wished to be left undisturbed in their less legitimate festivities.

The ship's Christmas duty had been predictable and, for the past two weeks or more, in anticipation, most of the men had been bottling their grog. It was a forbidden practice, but one not easy to prevent. While neat rum kept well, however, diluted rum — grog — did not. The traditional artifice was to add raisins to the bottle, which became swollen with the constituent water and were subsequently removed. The result was not quite neat rum, but it was almost so.

The hatch was closed, bottles emerged from lockers, and cups appeared. There was a tasting exchange in which vintages were compared and loudly defended. The air became progressively fume-laden and mess-deck life was suddenly rosy-hued. Stoker Bowles swung from the hammock bars, and Perk and Walt offered Crown and Anchor facilities. ERA Gilbert sang a song titled 'This Old Hat of Mine' which required him to jump up and down on SBA Peach's hat, but Peach was being sick in the bowl of nuts and did not care. Lobby Ludd drank a tot of rum standing on his head, and everyone except Peach had a slice of black pudding.

A few tots later Stoker Bowles performed a tap dance with Ginger Rogers, who resembled the deck-mop, and SBA Peach recovered sufficiently to show the knitted gloves, scarf and balaclava helmet he had received in a parcel, and which everyone tried on. ERA Gilbert suggested a game of Fire Brigade, which would entail lowering a fire hose down the hatch of the Marines' mess, forward, and turning on the hydrant. Before they could agree who would drive the fire engine, Peach had smoked a cigar and was sick on the electric fire. Stoker Bowles, his equilibrium becoming progressively more unstable, sat on the deck so that, if he collapsed, he would do so comfortably.

*

A few minutes before 2300 the destroyer Le Commandant, flying the ensign of the Free French naval forces and patrolling thirteen miles due south of the Needles, transmitted an Immediate signal to Portsmouth W/T on 2450 kc/s, reporting the interception of two unidentified vessels approaching at high speed from the south-east. Operations HQ, however, were aware of the identity of the approaching craft. They were two Royal Navy MTBs returning to harbour from a sweep on the enemy side of the Channel, and within minutes Portsmouth radioed a reply to Le Commandant, ordering her to ignore the contact; the vessels were friendly.

It was a routine situation, to be logged and forgotten — but then, suddenly, it was no longer routine. Le Commandant transmitted a second signal. It was too late. She had opened fire in the darkness and the two craft had been destroyed.

In the wheel-house of LCF49 a half-dressed Lieutenant Turk read the intercepted signals with pursed lips. 'God rest ye merry, gentlemen,' he muttered, patted his pockets for his cigarettes, then accepted one from Telegraphist Henry. He had been about to turn in, having just left the wardroom where his subordinate officers were drinking to 'Wives and sweethearts, may they never meet!' He sighed. 'Well I don't think it's likely to involve us, Sparks, but — ' He halted as Henry's headphones teetered and the man turned to his receiver, reaching for his morse key. 'Operational Priority, sir,' he said, 'for us — *VBQ v MTN-OP — 252328z GR22 ...* '

One minute later they were sharing the brief task of resolving the twenty-two groups of Fleet Code, and Turk swore softly.

'*LCF(L)49 from C-in-C Portsmouth: Operational Priority: Le Commandant's 252254z. Slip and proceed at utmost speed to position indicated. Investigate and report.*'

*

The moon was hidden by heavy cloud, the night black with thin flurries of snow as LCF49 slipped her lines and nosed into mid-stream. The few tiny, dim pools of light under the masked dockside lamps disappeared astern in seconds; the darkness closed around the ship with intimidating swiftness. All four officers were on the bridge, and on the foredeck the Marines were still struggling into duffel-coats and gloves. On after-deck and bows the seamen coiled down ropes and stared at the blackness to starboard. To the far, Hythe side of the fairway were several anchored oil barges and water lighters to which they must pass very close if they were to avoid the risk of collision with vessels that might be coming from seaward, and there was Hythe pier, which might carry lights and it might not. A few moments' error of only a degree or two would be disastrous, and there was ten miles of this confined, dark waterway before the wider Solent was reached.

Turk increased from slow to half speed. 'Number One,' he ordered, 'I want you forward with a couple of look-outs. As soon as we've cleared Netley I'm increasing to full ahead, so if we're going to hit anything you'll be the first to know. Give me a loud shout before you die at your post.' Visibility was barely a hundred yards.

'Shave off,' Perk said. 'If yer see the bleedin' Queen Mary, Walt, mind yer fingers.' He hawked and spat into the black void below the bows. 'Trust the soddin' French to make a cock-up — if it was a cock-up.'

There was a pervading distrust in the activities, even the integrity, of the Free French naval forces, perhaps born of resentment towards France's surrender and subsequent collaboration with the enemy, the U-boats' use of the Biscay bases and the denial of others to the British by armed force. It all added up to treachery, and if some Frenchmen could be treacherous, so could the others. There were many who refused to believe that the big FFNF submarine Surcouf had been sunk in collision with an American freighter. It was more likely that she had been killed by British destroyers because, it was said, allied ships had a distressing habit of disappearing in Surcouf's patrol area, and it was too much of a coincidence.

'There's Netley,' Turk decided, peering at the darkness to port. 'What do you think, Ludd?'

'Yessir,' Lobby Ludd agreed. 'That's Netley.' But that wasn't the bleedin' point. In this chilling game of blind-man's-buff a speed of only six knots was too fast. To increase to eleven knots was reckless.

Turk spoke into the wheel-house voice-pipe. 'Full ahead both.' From the voice-pipe came the telegraph's chang-chang and the coxswain's echoing voice. 'Full ahead both. Both engines full ahead, sir. Wheel amid-ships.' Underfoot, the deck began to tremble.

Lieutenant Bunter coughed nervously. He had a cold-clogged nose. 'I say, sir — isn't this a bit fast?'

'Well,' Lieutenant Taplow contributed, 'perhaps it's a bit fast — '

'I'm going to turn well inside the Calshot light vessel,' Turk said. 'That'll take us clear of any incoming shipping, and it'll save us twenty minutes. We're only drawing four and a half feet, and if we're lucky there'll be two fathoms under us. If we're unlucky, Summers is going to get a bloody shock.'

Calshot, Lobby Ludd remembered. Less than two years before the light cruiser Daemon, racing desperately for the Channel to engage Scharnhorst and Gneisenau, had skirted the Calshot shallows too closely and had run aground, earning her captain a court martial. But, then Daemon drew more than fourteen feet —

'If Commandant's gunnery is as good as she thinks,' Turk went on, 'there'll be two dozen men in the sea — if they've survived. Those MTBs are wooden-built and petrol-fuelled, so they burn like blazes. Any casualties will be taken straight below to the forward mess-deck, where the SBA will be waiting. Bunter, warn your Marines what they're looking for, and stand by to let go the cork rafts. Taplow, get the galley preparing something hot, please.' He paused. 'If those MTBs were doing anything like forty knots, the Frenchmen must have been bloody smart to have caught 'em.'

There was no crash, no screech of steel. There was hardly a jolt. LCF49's hull had been designed to run smoothly aground, and she did so now. It was as if a giant hand had grasped her in the darkness and drawn her firmly to a halt. She shivered a little as her screws threshed, pushing her square bows hard into the muddy bottom, and then she lay still.

Turk shouted profanities, shouted at the coxswain for full astern, rang the engine-room for every ounce of shaft thrust that the hammering diesels could generate, but LCF49 remained with her bows firmly embedded. It was blackly dark, very cold, and it was one o'clock on Boxing Day morning.

'W/T to bridge,' It was the telegraphist's voice. 'From Portsmouth, sir, Red Needles.'

'Sod the Needles,' Turk gritted. 'Number One! Are you there! Now, listen — and listen carefully, because if you don't get it right, we're all in the bloody cactus. I want you to clear lower deck of every mother's son in this ship that's not at an essential station. Get them all back aft — right aft — and start them all jumping in unison. Simultaneously, I'll go full astern again. I've seen it done once with a seven-hundred-ton trawler in the Schelde, so it ought to work with us. All right? Then move, Number One.'

They crowded aft in the darkness — sixty Marines, a handful of seamen, the ordnance artificer and the wireman, Bunter and Taplow — stumbling blindly over the stretched kedge-hawser and into each other, swearing. Summers climbed on to the capstan. 'Stand by to jump when I say so,' he shouted. 'Are you ready?' He drew a deep breath. 'Jump! Jump! Jump!'

*

On the deserted forward mess-deck SBA Peach laid out his rubber sheets, blankets, splints, tourniquets, morphine ampoules, tetanus antitoxin, Acriflavine and Dettol, then pulled a surgical gown over his arms. It was a laborious procedure he had carried out, or at least begun, on every occasion the ship had gone to action stations, and in a few minutes, no doubt, he would embark on the equally laborious procedure of packing everything back into the big, grey medicine chest. Peach had a grinding headache and his mouth was foul.

He was alone and it was very quiet — quiet, that is except for the faint noise of the engines that surged aft, and had now stopped. Minutes before the sergeants had ordered out every man. They had gone, cursing, and he had heard their shouts and the clatter of their feet on the deck above, but now there was silence, and he was alone. A door swung gently on its hinges and groaned. The lap of the sea against the ship's hull was just audible.

It was very odd, Peach thought, how everyone had so hurriedly abandoned the mess-deck. Nobody ever told him anything. Abandoned?

He frowned, straining his ears. Was that the sea only lapping against the ship's hull, or was it climbing the side? He felt his stomach twist. No, they wouldn't leave him here, would they?

Peach began to refold the blankets, then decided to inflate his life-belt and secure it firmly around his middle. Just in case. He could swear the deck was slightly tilted. If something was happening, there was no point in wearing an inflated life-belt down here, was there?

Hastily he thrust through the heavy, black canvas screen that shrouded the ladder and climbed his way to the upper deck. It was cold, and the night so black that he could not see his own hands on the hatch coaming.

He listened. From far aft he could hear the stamping of many feet, oaths, but above all a voice was shouting urgently.

'*Jump! Jump! Jump!*'

Peach knew. He choked, stumbled for the nearest rail, groping for it. My God, they'd forgotten him. His cotton gown caught on a stanchion, but he wrenched himself free, flung himself into a black abyss, holding his nose.

The sea was so icily cold that he yelled with the shock of it. His mouth filled with caustic brine and he thrashed wildly, kicking. The ship's side, grey in the dark, loomed above him, and he must get clear, he knew, before she went, or he would be dragged down with her. If he didn't die of cold first. Where was everyone else?

He trod water desperately, gasping, then stubbed a toe. He stretched down his legs tentatively and, incredulous, found himself standing upright. The sea was only four feet deep.

*

Inch by inch, LCF49 eased herself astern until her bows shuddered free of the mud and she floated clear. A ragged cheer came from the afterdeck and the hammer of jumping feet died.

'Thank Christ for that,' Turk breathed. 'We'll get out of here on tiptoe, arse first. Ludd, tell the First Lieutenant to secure aft.'

'*W/T to bridge. From C-in-C Portsmouth, sir. Cancel my 252328z. MTBs have passed Gilkicker Point and reported undamaged. Return to harbour.*'

Turk swore. 'Well, I'll be buggered — '

'*W/T to bridge. From Portsmouth, sir. White Needles.*'

'White balls,' Turk snorted.

Noisily disgruntled, the seamen regained their mess, peeling off their oilskins and blowing on cold fingers. Walt decided to make a kettle of tea.

'Sod this fer a skylark,' Perk panted. 'If I'd known there was going ter be runnin' and jumpin' games. I'd 'ave worn my soddin' shorts.'

Then Stoker Bowles, who was steaming his socks at the electric fire, said, 'Gawd strewth!'

SBA Peach blinked miserably in the light. His hair was wetly plastered over his face, his lips were blue and his teeth chattered. His torn and sodden surgical gown dripped water over muddy feet festooned with seaweed. He drooled.

'O' course,' he retorted bitterly, 'don't none of you worry about me. Don't you worry about a bloke that was bleedin' near drowned, will yer? I mean, you jus' drink yer soddin' tea. If I hadn't 'ad the presence o' mind — '

'I warned yer, Peachey,' Perk said. 'Never sit on the bog when we're goin' full revs, mate. I know. With bogs like them, I shouldn't be surprised if we all clew up with piles.'

Peach was being sick in the fire bucket.

*

Lobby Ludd's pink letters were becoming more menacing. She was not too upset, Freda Harris wrote, about the lack of an engagement ring. She would love one, of course, but it was something that, in wartime, many engaged couples dispensed with. Later, after they were married, he could give her an eternity ring. She was thinking about June. Could he get leave for June? In due course there were the banns to arrange — and whom did he want for his best man? Did he have a special friend, or would he like Owen Melville, who worked in the Borough Engineer's Department at the town hall? There were so many arrangements to discuss, and it might be a good idea for her to come down to Southampton for a day. She could meet some of his friends ...

'Yer'd think fighting a bleedin' war was enough,' Lobby Ludd complained, 'without 'aving yer morale undermined like this. Why's she want ter come ter soddin' Southampton?'

'She's going ter get yer ter sign them banns, mate,' Walt said. 'Once yer've signed them banns, yer finished. Before yer can say kiss my arse, yer up before the magistrate, payin' three quid a week fer bleedin' life.'

'And all yer can plead,' Perk added, 'is that the balance of yer mind was disturbed. Then they put yer away.'

*

At the gang-plank Marine Gilfedder, in belt, gaiters and side-arms, had just piped midday cooks to the galley when he found himself addressed by a slight, middle-aged lady on the jetty, clutching a handbag and a green umbrella. She wore her hair in a neat bun under a hat decorated with puce rose-buds and, around her neck, a length of ancient fur that terminated in a small, pointed snout and glass eyes.

'Young man,' she enquired, 'is this LCF49?'

It was difficult to understand how Mrs Ludd had progressed beyond the dockyard gate, where the security police could call upon sufficient resources to halt a Panzer regiment, but probably the sight of the little lady with her handbag and umbrella marching determinedly past the sandbags and barbed wire had paralysed all argument. Marine Gilfedder was six feet tall. 'Yes, ma'am,' he agreed, 'but — '

'You ought to be nearer to the station,' Mrs Ludd accused him. 'I had to get a bus.' Marine Gilfedder assumed an apologetic expression. 'I've come to see Charlie Ludd,' she explained and cautiously mounted the gang-plank.

'Charlie — ?' Marine Gilfedder frowned. 'Ah, yer must mean Lobby Ludd, our bunting-tosser. Well — I'm not sure, ma'am — ' But Mrs Ludd was already aboard. 'That thing's not very safe,' she said. 'I could easily have fallen off.'

'If yer'll just wait here, ma'am,' he suggested anxiously, 'I'll make enquiries.' There was nothing in his orders about elderly ladies with umbrellas. 'Yer see, it ain't usual — '

'No, don't you worry, young man,' she smiled. 'I'm going to give him a nice surprise. I have been on a ship before, you know — to the Isle of Man.' She fumbled in her handbag, found a sixpence, then smiled again. 'Charlie hasn't the faintest idea I'm coming.'

Marine Gilfedder stared at the sixpence in his hand, then looked up. 'No, ma'am!' he protested. 'Not down there. That's the wardroom.' He groaned resignedly.

Lieutenant Turk was about to climb the wardroom ladder when he came face to face with Mrs Ludd, who was descending with great care. 'Er — ' he said, and retreated backwards, hurriedly.

She beamed. 'Ah, if you'll just take my bag, young fellow — ' She reached the last rung gratefully. 'Those are very steep stairs, aren't they? I wear an elastic stocking, you know. It's my veins.' She straightened her hat.

Sub-Lieutenant Summers was in the process of pouring gins for himself, Bunter and Taplow. At Mrs Ludd's entrance, followed by Lieutenant Turk with her handbag, he froze. Bunter and Taplow scrambled to their feet, surprised. Mrs Ludd looked around the wardroom.

'This is very nice,' she approved. 'It's small, but very nice.'

Lieutenant Turk cleared his throat politely. 'Have you — er I mean, you haven't lost your way, ma'am? We don't often have ladies — '

'It's a surprise,' she said. 'I was just sitting and thinking, and I said to myself, "If it's a nice day tomorrow, I'll give Charlie a surprise." I haven't had a day out of the shop for years.' She decided to confide. 'I've got a little sweet shop, you know, in Walham Green, just off the North End Road — and I thought, as it was early closing, that I'd come down to see his ship. It doesn't take long from Waterloo, and that nice young soldier upstairs let me on.' She paused. 'I can't wait to see Charlie's face.'

The four officers gazed at her. 'Charlie?' Turk enquired.

'Charlie Ludd, of course,' she emphasized. 'I'm Mrs Ludd.'

Comprehension dawned. 'Ah — I see,' Lieutenant Turk nodded gravely, then smiled. 'Well, welcome aboard, Mrs Ludd. I think that "nice young soldier upstairs" may have mistaken you for one of the Wrens from the base, in civilian clothes — but it's not important. I am Lieutenant Turk, commanding. Please allow me to introduce my officers' — he turned — 'Sub-Lieutenant Summers, and Lieutenants Bunter and Taplow of the Royal Marines.'

Mrs Ludd shook the hand of each vigorously, then unpinned her fur tippet. 'I have been on a ship before, you know,' she told them, 'to the Isle of Man.' She glanced at the drinks cabinet. 'Of course, it had a big bar room, but I don't suppose you have the same crowds. And you could get sandwiches.'

'Yes — well — ' Turk frowned. 'Er — perhaps you would care for a drink? I'll send aft for Leading Signalman Ludd, and then — '

'That would be very nice,' Mrs Ludd agreed. 'I usually have a stout, or a port-and-lemon.' She seated herself firmly in the chair recently occupied by Lieutenant Bunter.

'I'm afraid', Summers apologized, 'we don't have much of a range. In fact, we mostly confine ourselves to Scotch and gin — or there's a little brandy — '

She considered. 'I'll start with a gin and tonic, young man,' she nodded, and looked around again. 'What you need is some nice wallpaper, to hide all those nails, and a few curtains. Ah, thank you, young man. God bless. It's a pity you're so far from the station. Still, now I know where you are, I can come again.' She paused. 'And where's the "Ladies"?'

Lieutenant Turk was having difficulty in maintaining a politely serious expression. 'Excuse me,' he murmured, and retreated to the pantry. 'Steward!' he hissed. 'Go aft and get Leading Signalman Ludd — at the rush!'

Only a few minutes earlier, however, Stoker Bowles had reached the mess with the corned beef surprise and the jam clacker. 'Lobby,' he said, 'there's a party come aboard, arsking for yer. I jest 'eard her talking ter that ginger-'aired bootneck on the gang-plank.'

'A party?' Lobby Ludd gaped. 'Fer me?'

Stoker Bowles nodded. 'And she's gone down ter the wardroom.'

'I told yer, mate,' Walt pronounced. 'Yer've 'ad yer chips. I bet she's got a court order — '

'But I ain't even bought a ring,' Lobby Ludd protested. 'That don't matter.' Perk shook his head. 'It's what yer said like Errol Flynn. Was there any witnesses?'

Lobby Ludd was not entirely convinced. 'Was she about as tall as this?' he asked Stoker Bowles, holding his hand as high as his nose, 'and a brunette?'

'Well,' Stoker Bowles estimated, 'I suppose yer might call 'er a brunette.' He was intrigued. 'She ain't your party, is she?' There was no accounting for it. He sniffed. 'Shave off.'

'She ain't that bad,' Lobby Ludd snorted, nettled. 'I might tell yer there was quite a few blokes in Fulham chasin' 'er before I scored, mate, and it took a lot o' chat. She played 'ard ter get.'

'Shave off,' Stoker Bowles repeated, amazed, but decided that there was such a thing as diplomacy. 'O' course, looks ain't everything,' he conceded, but the situation in Fulham must be desperate.

Perk knew his law. 'If she's going ter serve a summons, Lobby, she's got ter serve it personal, see. Otherwise it don't count,' He calculated. 'If you was in the paint locker, say, and nobody knew — I mean — she can't stay on board for bleedin' ever. I read about a bloke that was called up for the army, and hid in a privy at the bottom o' the garden fer three soddin' years, until he died o' pneumonia. When they found him, he was jes' skin an' bone.'

'Bleedin' marvellous,' Lobby Ludd gritted, but there was not much time. 'All right — and don't bleedin' forget I'm down there.' The paint locker hatch was secured from the outside.

*

Mrs Ludd gave her empty glass to Sub-Lieutenant Summers for the third time. 'Not so much tonic this time, young man,' she suggested. 'It's a crime to drown it, I always say. Do you have any lemon or ice?' Summers regretted he did not; lemons were unobtainable and the ship did not have a refrigerator. The steward returned to report that he had been unable to find Leading Signalman Ludd anywhere, and nobody seemed to know where he was. 'Will the lady be staying for lunch, sir?' he whispered.

'Don't you do anything special,' Mrs Ludd warned. 'I'll just have anything that's going.' Her hat had become slightly rakish, and she straightened it again. 'Did I tell you that I have been on a ship before? To the Isle of Man. I was sick all the way over, and sick all the way back.' She hiccuped, and put a genteel hand to her lips. 'Pardon me.'

'Number One.' Lieutenant Turk spoke from the corner of his mouth, urgently. 'Find Ludd.' Mrs Ludd eyed her empty glass and sighed. 'Charlie's just like his father,' she told Lieutenant Bunter. 'We lost him once, on Boat Race day, near Putney Bridge — Charlie, I mean, when he was small. Roland and me hadn't been in the Star and Garter for more than five minutes.' She put her glass into Bunter's hand. 'I'll have the same again, dear. I hope your waiter isn't going to any fuss. I don't mind sandwiches, or a slice of veal-and-ham — '

Sub-Lieutenant Summers looked on the bridge, peered into the wheelhouse, then descended to the seamen's mess-deck. 'Has anyone seen Ludd?' he asked.

'That's funny, sir,' Perk puzzled. 'The wardroom flunkey was arsking the same thing. He was 'ere, sir, but he ain't now.'

'He was 'ere,' Stoker Bowles agreed. 'If yer like, sir, I'll look in the engine-room — although I can't think why he should be in the engine-room — '

'Neither can I,' Summers snorted. 'Perkins — Walters — find Ludd. I don't care where he is, or what he's doing — just find him. Search forward, the galley, the magazine, look on the jetty, and see if he's on the ship alongside. Don't do anything else until he's found — and find him now.'

'It's like one o' them mysteries o' the sea,' Walt said. 'Suppose we never find 'im? Or suppose we only find'is skeleton be'ind the flag-locker?'

'Find Ludd!' Summers roared.

Fifteen minutes later, however, a frustrated First Lieutenant returned to the wardroom. 'I can't understand it,' he exclaimed. 'I just can't understand it.'

'I could,' Turk gritted, 'if he got a red alert. Under different circumstances I could almost sympathize.'

The hat with the puce rose-buds was raffishly askew, and Mrs Ludd patted Lieutenant Taplow's knee affectionately with a hand that held a cold beef sandwich. 'You're all good boys,' she asserted with slight difficulty. 'I've always liked sailors.' She waved the sandwich in the direction of Lieutenant Bunter. 'I'll come again. Not next week, but — ' She calculated, and Turk tensed, but she was unable to decide. 'And you must all come to Walham Green. Turn right when you come out of the station and cross over at the lights.' Taplow brushed the crumbs from his knee and Mrs Ludd looked for her glass.

Turk glanced at his watch. 'I think', he murmured to Summers, 'that the lady ought to go before she starts singing "Roll Out the Barrel". Number One, you'd better phone from the jetty for a taxi.'

Summers nodded, then hesitated. 'Sir, taxis are only permitted as far as the dockyard gate. Someone will have to go with her. Perhaps the coxswain — '

'No, Number One.' Turk smiled at Mrs Ludd, who was showing Lieutenant Bunter her elastic stocking. 'Never let it be said that the officers of LCF49 were guilty of the slightest discourtesy.' He turned his smile towards Summers. 'You will escort the lady to the dockyard gate, Number One. It comes under the heading of "miscellaneous duties not otherwise listed".'

'Sir — !' Summers pleaded.

'Give my love to Charlie,' Mrs Ludd instructed Lieutenant Turk, who promised that he would. 'I'll see him next time I come.' Turk's eyes were pained, but he still smiled. She negotiated the gang-plank apprehensively, steadied by Sub-Lieutenant Summers and Marine

Gilfedder, then turned to wave at the gathering of interested ship's company. 'It's been very nice,' she told everyone. 'Next time, I'll bring some lemons. I can always get a few lemons.' Her hat had fallen over one ear.

'I'd never 'ave believed it,' Stoker Bowles vowed, 'if I'adn't seen with my own eyes.'

Summers suggested to Mrs Ludd that it was unnecessary to raise her umbrella because it was not raining, but she insisted. It looked like it might rain. 'If you don't mind, young man,' she said, 'I'll take your arm. I can't think why there's railway lines where people have to walk.'

*

Both had disappeared from view for several minutes when Lieutenant Turk suddenly drew a deep breath and narrowed his eyes. 'Ludd — what a pity — you're just too late. We did search the ship for you, Ludd, but your visitor had to leave. I know you're disappointed.' He shook his head. 'But, just to satisfy an idle curiosity, where exactly were you?'

Lobby Ludd's face showed concern. 'Well, sir, I was tidyin' up in the paint locker — '

'Ah — the paint locker,' Turk nodded. 'Now, who would have thought to look in a paint locker with a door secured from the outside? It would have fooled anyone.'

'That's exactly what I said to myself, sir. It must have been the wind — and I found myself locked in. I hollered, o' course, but it didn't do no good. At first, I was afraid I might be there for weeks, but I kept calm. If yer get excited, yer use up oxygen. Sooner or later, I said, someone's going to want ter paint something. I must hold on. Then, jes' when I was beginning ter despair — '

'The wind blew again?' Turk suggested.

'Yes sir,' Lobby Ludd said, surprised. '"Ow did yer guess?'

*

'Number One,' Turk advised, 'tell Perkins to get cleaned out of that Wakefield Trinity shirt. I don't think Captain D will be impressed — he's probably an RFU man.'

Commander Bullock, RN, came aboard from Toreador, the crack destroyer out of Portsmouth, with that ship's gunnery officer and his personal Yeoman of Signals. All three climbed to the bridge, avoiding contact with the wet handrail, and gazed about them with the mildly pained eyes of men who really had no time to waste on shabby little assault vessels. The commander grunted an acknowledgement of Turk's salute, then stood at the screen with his head thrust forward and his hands behind his back. The gunnery officer toyed with a stopwatch on a lanyard, and the yeoman told Lobby Ludd that the flag-deck was downright filthy. Lobby Ludd refrained from replying that it was going to get filthier, any minute now.

'All right, Turk,' the commander nodded. 'You ought to know the drill. We'll engage the three cliff targets first, in succession, and see what sort of time you can put up. *Toreador's* best performance is one minute six seconds, and she averages one twenty one.' He sniffed.

They waited until, ashore, the red flags rose at each end of the firing-range. The targets were three white rectangles, each at a different distance and angle of sight, but high on the cliff face, small and indistinct against the background, chalk rubble. 'Stand by port battery,' Turk ordered. The first mile markers were directly abeam. 'Open fire.' The gunnery officer looked at his stop-watch with a smile and the commander raised his binoculars.

'Cease fire!' Turk shouted. The distant targets had disappeared in eruptions of white dust and the red flags were down. The gunnery officer frowned. 'Fifty-eight seconds,' he reported.

'You mean one minute fifty-eight seconds,' Commander Bullock corrected. He glared at the soot that speckled his immaculate shirt-cuffs, and fumbled for a handkerchief.

'No, sir,' the gunnery officer said, putting the stopwatch to his ear. 'Fifty-eight seconds.'

There was plainly a mistake but, annoyingly, Turk did not seem inclined to concede it. 'Shall we try the starboard battery on the reverse run, sir?' he said.

'Fifty-eight seconds is impossible,' the yeoman explained to Lobby Ludd. 'Nobody's done it faster'n *Toreador*.'

Lobby Ludd nodded. 'There's probably some bloke up there, with a grudge, kicking the targets down.'

'You'd better stand next to me, Gorman,' the commander told the gunnery officer. 'I want to keep an eye on that stopwatch.'

The red flags were fluttering at the cliff top. 'Stand by starboard battery,' Turk ordered, and waited for the mile markers to come into alignment. 'Open fire.' The commander's binoculars searched for the targets, obscured by a pall of chalk dust — first one, then the second, then the third. 'Cease fire!' Turk shouted.

'Stuff my tall hat,' the yeoman marvelled.

The gunnery officer gazed at the stop-watch for a long time. 'Fifty-seven seconds, sir,' he apologized.

Commander Bullock wiped soot from the creases of his neck. 'Well,' he grunted, 'I suppose you would shoot another hundred times, and never do it again. These sort of performances are always open to question. Consistency is the thing. We'll see what you can do with a towed surface target, Turk. The tug will be waiting for us off St Catherine's.' He paused. 'Now, there can't be any fluke about this, because we've devised a fool-proof system. The target consists of three independently floating trellis-and-canvas structures, each ten feet long by five high, towed at half-cable intervals. That means if there's anything like a swell you won't see much of them. When the tug fires a white flare you can start shooting. After exactly one minute the tug will fire a red flare, and you will stop immediately. Then the tug will count hits. Understand? Now, *Toreador* completely demolished two structures and actually got one shell into the third, which means she's capable of destroying two E-boats and damaging another in one minute.' He eyed his blackened handkerchief. 'Can't you do anything about that bloody chimney?'

'Don't E-boats go a bit faster than gunnery targets?' Lobby Ludd asked the yeoman. 'About forty knots faster?'

The LCF had cleared the Needles and the gunnery officer pointed. 'There she is, sir.' He had satisfied himself that his stop-watch ticked for sixty seconds in every minute. The wardroom steward was anxiously collecting the officers' coffee cups before the next shooting began.

'Are your guns quite ready?' Commander Bullock enquired. 'All right, Yeoman. Tell the tug we're waiting.' The Aldis lamp click-clacked and the distant tug acknowledged. 'I'm going ter keep my eyes on them targets,' the yeoman promised, 'jest in case.'

The white flare climbed skyward, twinkled, but had not reached the zenith of its trajectory when the ship's barrage exploded, and the commander, coughing, focussed his binoculars through another swirl of soot. On the fore-deck expended magazines were being wrenched from guns, fresh ones hammered home.

'Red flare, sir!' the yeoman yelled.

'Cease fire!' ordered Turk.

The tug was steering a wide circle and her lamp was blinking. 'All targets destroyed well within one minute. Am taking in tow. If you wish to continue I must return to Bembridge for replacements.'

Commander Bullock blew his nose loudly. 'Yeoman, tell the tug, "Exercise completed", then order *Toreador* alongside. I want a bath; I feel like Al Jolson — and, Gorman, we'd better take another look at this damn target drill. Floating incinerators don't shoot better than destroyers. Have a talk with Whale Island ... '

Five

With an almost sinister unobtrusiveness the signs were increasing. The invasion, earlier so nebulous because its massive dimensions were beyond the comprehension of ordinary men, was taking positive shape, and the inevitability of it was coldly sobering. Each newly emerging development provided another reminder that it was going to happen. Nobody, yet, could see the whole of it, but there were fragmentary glimpses of a vast, unfolding extravaganza that were often puzzling, sometimes discomforting. Every craft was one of a flotilla, each flotilla a member of an assault group, which in turn was only a segment of a naval force. The five forces — G, J, O, S and U — were deployed among the harbours of Falmouth, Fowey, Plymouth, Salcombe, Dartmouth, Brixham, Torbay, Portland, Weymouth, Poole, Exbury, the Solent and Spithead, Shoreham, Newhaven, Harwich and the Nore, and new ships were joining them almost daily. To exercise simultaneously the entire armada of six thousand craft was impossible; they would sail as one fleet only on the day of invasion, and when that happened the possibility of chaos was not remote. The control of only several hundred vessels presented problems. Following Channel manoeuvres they were dispersed to their various bases by means of a stratagem dubbed a 'sausage machine', but which more nearly resembled a vast clock-spring of ships unwinding for hours, far into the night.

As 1944 moved into February civilian travel between the UK and the Irish Republic — the base for an active enemy espionage network — was forbidden. Parks and heathlands throughout the south of England were becoming prohibited areas, cordoned by wire and stockpiled with stores and ammunition or mushroomed with prefabricated accommodation. Armed sentries patrolled serried lines of military vehicles. There were boats that ran on roads, tanks that swam, that flailed, that laid roads or lifted bridge sections. There were guns, gliders, ambulances and mobile kitchens. Wheels and tracks rumbled on every country road, and there were troops everywhere — British, American, Canadian, Polish, French. In several dockyards a number of old ships were being stripped and prepared for use as an off-shore breakwater, and two immense floating harbours, each with the capacity of Dover, were nearing completion.

The importance of other theatres of war had for the moment, paled. The Japanese tide had been halted in Burma, but Burma was far distant. The Italian campaign had bogged down at Cassino. The Russians had retaken Novgorod, but their offensive, too, would soon be slowed by the thaw. In the Pacific the Americans had destroyed Truk, taken Kwajalein, Engebi, Eniwetok and Parry.

*

'It'll be a bloody relief', one of the drinkers was saying as Lobby Ludd, Perk and Walt entered the Woolston bar, 'when all these service blokes bugger off on their invasion. Yer can't move for soldiers.'

'And I've got to take care of my regulars,' the publican nodded. He sniffed, wiped the bar top with a sodden cloth, and turned to the newcomers. 'No beer, only shandies.' Several of his customers pushed glasses behind elbows. 'Or there's Green Goddess or Fruit Cup, two an' six.'

Lobby Ludd considered. 'Ah, yes. Fourteen pints o' shandy, then, fer a start.'

'Fourteen? Fourteen pints?' The publican frowned. 'For three of you?'

'The others are jes' coming,' Lobby Ludd explained, glancing over his shoulder. ''Arf the ship's company, and the ship's cat.' He smiled. 'It's lucky we got 'ere before yer sold out.'

For several minutes the publican was occupied with the task of filling fourteen glasses with a mixture of beer and lemonade that was largely lemonade. The sailors watched gravely.

'And fourteen packets o' crisps,' Perk decided.

'I'll tell yer what,' Walt said. 'We'll 'ave three Green Goddesses while we wait, and chase 'em with shandies. Don't ferget the cherries on sticks, mate.'

'Make 'em navy size,' Lobby Ludd added, thrusting a hand into a pocket. 'How much is all that?'

The publican calculated. 'Fourteen shandies — that's twenty-one shillings. Three double Green Goddesses, fifteen shillings — '

'Hang on the slack, mate,' Lobby Ludd interrupted. 'These are lemonade shandies. We wanted ginger-beer shandies.'

'That's right,' Walt confirmed. 'Ginger-beer. I can't stand bleedin' lemonade.'

'None o' these crisps 'ave got salt in,' complained Perk, who had opened every packet. 'What's the good o' soddin' crisps with no salt in?'

'It's at the bottom,' the publican insisted. 'The salt's always at the bottom.'

'And when yer get to it', Perk snorted, 'yer've eaten orl the crisps.' He shook his head. 'I ain't having that.'

'Are you paying for this lot?' the publican gritted. 'It's two pounds an' eightpence.'

'Yer can scrub round the shandies,' Lobby Ludd said, and put his money back into his pocket. 'We don't want lemonade shandy. It ain't the same.'

'And we don't want crisps with no salt till yer've finished,' Perk shrugged. 'I'd rather 'ave nuts an' raisins.'

The publican stared at them. 'What about them Green Goddesses?'

'They're green,' Walt shuddered. 'I never knew they was green. I thought that was jes' the name. I mean, Scotch eggs ain't Scotch, are they? Or soddin' Welsh rabbits? I couldn't fancy anything that's green, could you, Perk?'

The publican was unbelieving. 'What', he demanded, 'do you think I can do with all this?' He indicated the crowded bar top.

They glanced at each other, and Lobby Ludd grinned. 'Well ... '

*

In April, in the UK, security precautions were tightened even further. Foreign diplomats and couriers were forbidden to leave or enter the country. Diplomatic mail was censored. All non-military travellers were denied access to within ten miles of the coast between Land's End and the Wash, and both sides of the Firth of Forth. Britain had become a silent, armed camp. An invasion was about to be launched, and the Germans knew it. What they did not know — only a very few people in Britain knew — were the day, the time and the place.

May was sunny, blue-skied and mild, and all that month the long convoys of trucks and tanks moved southward, with the soldiers waving and shouting at the girls as they passed. The towns of tents multiplied, and more and more landing craft jockeyed for position in Southampton Water, pushing their bows up the hard aprons from which they would embark. British and American aircraft were being painted with black and white zebra stripes on wings and fuselage to facilitate recognition. There was an uneasy awareness now that a colossal monster had been set into motion and could not be stopped, that it was gathering speed with every day. Hundreds of thousands of men in camps and messdecks waited, impatient but apprehensive, cleaned their weapons, checked ammunition, tuned engines, then tuned them again, played cards, joked nervously. Would the time never come?

May ended in a final crescendo of sunshine, but the first day of June, Thursday, was overcast and chilly, with the harbour waters stippled by wind. There had been a flurry of activity among the flotilla's commanding officers, briefings, worried faces, the arrival of new charts, code-books, the installation of a new VHF radio-telephone on every bridge. On Saturday the third Lieutenant Turk ordered the ship's company to muster on the forward mess-deck, and an expectant hum died as he pinned up a chart. He turned to face them.

'From this moment,' he said, 'all hands are confined to the ship. Nobody will go on shore, for any reason, without my express permission.' He paused. 'Tomorrow, subject to weather conditions, Force J will rendezvous with other invasion components in mid-Channel, and then proceed to the French coast, arriving at dawn on Monday. You all know what that means.'

There was complete silence.

'The flotilla', he resumed, 'will accompany the assault of the Third Canadian Infantry Division and the Second Canadian Armoured Brigade, which will land on Juno Beach — covering Courseulles, Bemferes and St Aubin.' He pointed at the chart, but the names were meaningless.

'I cannot tell you what will happen there. Your guess is as good as mine. I do know that the enemy defences will have been subjected to intensive bombardment by our heavy units before we hit the beach, but there may still remain considerable enemy fire-power. Our job is to get the troops ashore with as few casualties as possible, and that means that our own fortunes are of secondary importance. We are expendable.' He grinned.

'There will be no mail going ashore. When we slip tomorrow it's going to be a long night and an even longer day to follow, so wear comfortable clothes and shoes' — he grinned again — 'carpet-slippers, if you like.

And before we start, change into clean underclothes. During the operation I will try to keep you supplied with information and news. Meanwhile, I suggest you all get an early night; it could be your last for some time.'

It could be your last, he thought.

*

The assault groups that had harboured in the ports of Devon, largely American, had already sailed for the Channel rendezvous at dawn on Sunday, 4 June, thrusting into a grey, torn sea and a rising wind that tugged at barrage balloons and streamed the coloured signal bunting from swaying mastheads. Many heavy units — battleships, cruisers, monitors and destroyers — had left their anchorages in Scapa Flow, the Firth of Forth, the Clyde and Belfast, and were at sea. Elsewhere, along the entire length of the south coast, the invasion fleet was fully embarked and ready to slip, the laden ships rising and falling at jetties, pulling at their buoys, packed with a hundred thousand troops, many of whom had been aboard for days. There was sea-sickness and misery in the crowded, confined decks, and still the weather worsened, with a gale warning at 11 a.m. All hope of a landing on a storm-lashed French coast within the next twenty-four hours had drained.

The convoy that struggled up-Channel from westward was recalled. The battered little craft huddled in Weymouth Bay, their human cargoes soaked, cold and dispirited. Everything had been planned to the last detail, except one thing — the weather.

For weeks, months, they had thought about it, superficially discussed it, some with bravado and others swallowing on misgivings. Opinions on the pattern of events that might be expected had differed, but there was a logical, if over-simplified, sequence — the Channel crossing, the assault on a fortified shore, then the campaign inland. The third of these phases was precisely planned. Every combat unit had its objectives specified for D-Day, for D plus one, plus two, even for weeks after the initial landings, and yet it was impossible for most men to think clearly beyond the second phase, beyond the high-water mark of a French beach. If they survived that, what followed would take care of itself — or the top brass would take care of it. They had become mentally attuned only to that brief, explosive experience of a bow-ramp crashing open and a crouching, panting, scrambling advance over rocks and sand, with men scythed down and the survivors blaspheming, grateful for life. If they were still alive, nothing else much mattered.

And it was going to happen tomorrow morning, but now it was not.

*

In Fort Southwick on Portsdown Hill, above Portsmouth, there had been several days of agonizing indecision among the small group of men who headed the Allied Command for Operation Overlord — the invasion of the European mainland of which Operation Neptune was the landing phase. Monday the fifth, Tuesday the sixth and Wednesday the seventh were the only days during June when both Channel tides and available moonlight were suitable for all the many aspects of the enterprise. A postponement of one day, possibly two, was acceptable, but after that the thousands of men in the cramped ships would have to be disembarked — but they could not be returned to their camps because these were already occupied by follow-up divisions. Furthermore, thousands had been briefed, ashore and afloat, plans and charts had been distributed, everyone knew too much, and a delay of more than hours would mean that compromise was a certainty. The monster had been set into motion. It must either go forward or it would collapse.

Then, on the evening of Sunday, within an hour of the deadline for a second, probably final, postponement, meteorologists reported an approaching brief break in the bad weather. Conditions would improve that night and would continue fair until dawn on Tuesday, after which they would again deteriorate. The opportunity offered was perilously thin, but it had to be taken.

The decision was unanimous. The invasion was on.

From the yard-arm of the monitor Roberts, moored below Woolston, a medley of coloured flags fluttered in the wind 'God speed and give them hell'.

*

It was late afternoon of Monday, 5 June, and for several hours Southampton had been emptying line after line of ships and landing craft into the Solent, southward, and LCF49 led the brood of squat LCFs and LCGs into the fairway. All hands except those in engine-room and wheel-house were on deck, savouring the moment, with feelings that none would sensibly analyse later — a turmoil of elation, awe and apprehension that tingled on the tongue like hot curry and contorted the belly. Everyone grinned and there was an exchange of nervous, juvenile banter. Lieutenant Bunter had brought the wardroom gramophone to the bridge and was attempting to play 'Anchors Aweigh' through the microphone of the loud hailer, but was achieving only a deafening screech. Everyone roared with laughter. Lobby Ludd, earlier, had changed into clean underclothes and then, on impulse, donned his number one, best blue suit with gold badges, tailored by Bernard's, and his best shoes and cap. If he was going to get his come-uppance, he decided, he would get it in his best suit and, if he survived, he would gladly buy another. When he reached the bridge he observed that Lieutenant Turk, at the compass platform, was also wearing his best suit of black doeskin and an immaculate cap. They eyed each other, and both grinned, knowing. 'Up pennants, Ludd,' Turk nodded, 'and hoist our battle ensign.' He had acquired a huge white ensign, probably intended for a battleship, and had been saving it for this day. It was vast, snowy white, with red and blue congealing, proud and beautiful against the sullen, grey sky.

Perk and Walt, with hands thrust into duffel-coat pockets, stood at the two twin Lewis gun mountings abaft the bridge, and ERA Gilbert's head protruded from the engine-room hatch. Towing astern were two forty-foot motorboats, converted assault landing craft, now LCA(HR), or Landing Craft Assault, Hedgerow, each carrying a crew of four. With strengthened hull frames, the boats were armed with twenty-four mortars in four rows of six. When released from their tow they would dash ahead of the assault fleet, volley their mortar-bombs to explode among the beach mine-fields, and then retire. Now, as the massive, closely formed convoy moved out of the comparative shelter of Southampton Water into the open Solent, and then Spithead, the two small craft in the wake of LCF49 began to rear and plunge in the vicious swell. It was dusking. To port was Stokes Bay, Southsea and the lonely hump of Spit Fort. To starboard, distant, was Ryde Pier and a purple headland. Ahead was the sentinel Nab lightship, rolling, and the open Channel. It was cold, with a gusting wind, the tang of funnel smoke in the nostrils, the smell of warm oil, the galley cooking, and the throb of living engines underfoot. There was no going back now. 'The die is cast!' said SBA Peach, striking a Hamlet pose, and Stoker Bowles told him to shit in it. Peach went forward to unpack the big, grey medicine chest and lay out his rubber sheets, blankets and splints. When the shooting began, he decided, he could lie down between the mess tables. He was, after all, entitled to protection under the Geneva Convention. The deck was rolling uncomfortably and, as a precaution, he took two hyoscine hydrobromide tablets, which made him feel sick.

Turk was mildly concerned that almost none of the ship's company showed any desire to leave the upper deck for very long. He had ordered one watch to stand down, but he could hardly compel men to sleep. Despite a gusting south-westerly gale, a nasty sea and occasional rain swells, they remained doggedly at their action stations. A few drifted away to brew tea or doze on a mess-stool, only to awaken guiltily in minutes and scramble for the ladder. Above, they stood at their guns, or in small groups, shoulders hunched and talking quietly. Ahead, astern and on both sides the invasion fleet stretched as far as the eye could see in the semi-darkness, and sometimes there was the drone of aircraft overhead. Presumably they were friendly or, again presumably, there would be a broadcast warning, but all radio frequencies were silent. Port wave, maintained by Portsmouth and Portland, was functioning as if the night was no different to any other.

It was becoming inconceivable, however, that the enemy was still unaware of the thousands of ships milling around in the Channel. A night air attack of any significance was considered unlikely, and the protective screen, if out of sight, of seven battleships, twenty-seven cruisers and two hundred destroyers was probably impenetrable, but there must surely have been, by now, some sightings, either surface, air or radar, or some security betrayal. Parachute and glider troops would begin landing in enemy territory soon after midnight; the enemy would then have six hours in which to mobilize resources to oppose the seaborne assault.

*

For an hour or more there had been a suspicion of faint flashing against the dark horizon beyond the bows, but nobody was really sure. Soon after 0500, however, there was no longer any doubt, and Summers noted it in the deck log. The sky was just beginning to pale, and everyone was now at his station, peering ahead. It was impossible to determine whether the flashes were of bombs or shell-fire. Several men claimed they could hear the rumble of explosions, but it was doubtful. Some of the larger flashes illuminated momentarily the blanket of cloud overhead and silhouetted the surrounding ships. As the sky pearled they could recognize several of the larger vessels around them — the landing ships Prince David, Prince Henry and Prince Baudouin, the headquarters ship Hilary. There were scores of landing craft of every type, smashing their ramped bows into the swell, and smaller, towed craft plunging and bucking. Everything, suddenly, was beginning to happen. 'Speed signal, sir,' Lobby Ludd shouted. 'Ten knots.'

There was a coastline ahead, indistinct yet, but overlaid by drifting smoke and pitted with tiny flickers of light. The sea in every direction was crowded with ships racing for that irregular grey reef in the distance which was France. Turk was mouthing orders to the wheel-house, glancing astern at the flotilla that followed, then at the Hedgerow craft below with their huddled, clinging crewmen. To port, a mile away and shrouded in her own gun-smoke, was the battleship Warspite, with attendant destroyers. Her guns erupted, and the flight of the fifteen-inch shells was clearly visible, like dully glowing sparks in the half-light. Nearer were two rocket-mounted LCTs, each carrying more than a thousand high-explosive five-inch rockets intended to be electrically fired in twenty-four salvoes at a fixed range of 3,500 yards. The massed missiles screamed skyward, salvo after salvo in a paroxysm of flame, to coincide brutally with the overhead flight of three Spitfires, swooping coastward, and obliterate them instantly. Aircraft fragments tumbled to the sea. 'Shave off,' Walt said, and rolled himself a tickler with damp fingers.

Nobody gave the mishap more than a quick glance before forgetting it — the tiniest of details in a vast, panoramic canvas in which so many things were happening simultaneously. If the Germans had earlier been slow to understand the real meaning of the pre-dawn thunder from the north-west, they were reacting now. The ragged white plumes of falling shells, perhaps probing for Warspite, were bursting in the sea. Many of the falls were obscured from view, but a light cruiser had sustained a hit and was vomiting smoke. On LCF's fore-deck the Oerlikon gunners were strapped into their guns and the two-pounders were turning their muzzles. 'All guns loaded and ready, sir,' Bunter reported. He wore working khaki and his only accessory was a small megaphone with which to shout orders at the gun crews. Taplow was at the magazine hatch.

The nearer landing ships were lowering assault craft, packed with troops, from their gravity davits into a swell that clutched them roughly and whirled them off as their screws churned. 'LCAs away, sir,' Lobby Ludd shouted, although Turk could see for himself. The little boats had seven miles of sea to cover before they achieved the shore, and it was going to be a shuddering experience for the men crouched in their narrow well-decks. Overhead, more aircraft screamed shoreward. There seemed to be smoke everywhere.

'Let go the Hedgerows,' Turk ordered, and Lobby Ludd repeated the instruction over the loud-hailer. 'Let go Hedgerows aft.'

The towed boats had been shipping water for hours, with their crews baling.

'Have yer got a match, Perk?' Walt asked. 'Mine's soddin' wet.' He glanced at his fellow. 'What's up, mate? Yer been hit already? Shave off, we've only jes' bleedin' started.'

Perk was cradling his jaw in both hands. 'Soddin' toothache,' he gritted. 'Yer don't suppose — if I arsked — that the skipper would send me off ter get a fillin'? I mean, I suppose there's 'ospital ships, ain't there?'

Walt was doubtful. 'Arsk 'im when yer've shot down a Messerschmidt,' he suggested.

From the after-deck Summers had signalled to the two mortar craft that they should cast off their ropes. One did so, falling astern as her engine fired sluggishly, but then increasing speed and turning away. The other, however, was less fortunate. Its youthful sub-lieutenant shouted that his craft was almost water-logged, the engine-space was flooded and the engine dead. Summers was uncertain, but Turk's angry voice was flaring over the loud-hailer.

'Number One! Get rid of that bloody boat, will you? We're increasing speed to engage. If he won't let go, turn him adrift.'

The officer in the wallowing mortar craft was still shouting but his words were lost in the general noise. Summers and a seaman wrested the rope from its bollard and flung it astern, free of the LCF's screws. Released, the mortar craft slowed, twisting and plunging helplessly. Then a massive roller lifted it high and toppled it over, keel upward, into the following trough. Smoke closed over it, and in seconds the capsized boat was lost to sight.

'When yer think about it,' Walt sympathized, 'he needn't really 'ave come. He could 'ave stayed at 'ome and listened ter it on the wireless.'

The long, irregular strand of the French coast ahead was nearing, and recognizable features were assuming shape through the gaps in the drifting smoke. There were church towers, a tall narrow chimney, rooftops, trees, sand dunes. It was difficult to believe that this was really occupied France. Through binoculars it was possible to see the rollers breaking against the beach, first a sandy foreshore and then a belt of shingle that climbed to a sea-wall. Beyond was a long row of houses, not unlike the boarding-houses of any English resort, but it was the beach that held all attention. The waves were high, splintering among half-submerged steel and concrete obstructions and festooned wire. Concrete bunkers with gun-slits were built against the sea-wall, and there was a scattering of pill-boxes reinforced by sandbags. All appeared to be unscathed; the pre-assault rocket bombardment was falling short, with several salvoes falling so closely ahead of the leading assault craft that they were swerving away to avoid the hundreds of exploding waterspouts. There was little evidence of damage from the heavy ships' earlier barrage, but the wreathing smoke made observation difficult. LCF49 was hammering through the sea at emergency full speed, pouring black smoke from her funnel, astern of her the assault flotilla, on both sides, like eager ducklings, the dozens of cockle-shell craft tightly crowded with infantrymen, heads bowed against the stinging spray. From the nearest came the sound of singing, and the words were French. They were men of the Canadian Queen's Own Rifles, and many, as they sang, vomited into the paper bags issued for the purpose. At a thousand yards there was floating wreckage and capsized hulls, a tangle of corpses tossed aside by the ship's bow wave, men swimming desperately, shouting hopelessly. Eight hundred yards.

The houses that were like a terrace of English boardinghouses had windows resembling empty eye-pits, and there were shattered roofs. The beaches were ominously nearer, still hazed by distracting smoke. The houses must be Bernières. There were shallows here, according to the chart, and underwater outcrops of rock that could tear the bottom out of a small craft, but the tide was high. Christ, it was high. More shells were bursting in the sea. Whose? And a string of eruptions along the beach — six, seven — but they were too late; in seconds the leading assault craft would be grounding, the men ashore. A blow like a massive fist met LCF49 full in the bows. The ship shuddered, lowered her nose into a lake of white froth, then reared and lurched on through yet more smoke, seemingly unhurt.

'That was a near miss,' Turk shouted. 'Number One, check forward for damage, please.'

Six hundred yards, and closing.

'DD tanks launching, sir,' Lobby Ludd advised. Astern, following LSTs had stopped with opened bow doors, and amphibious Duplex Drive Sherman tanks were taking the water like fat brown beetles, wallowing uncomfortably in the heavy swell. In moments several had disappeared completely, failing to survive their first plunging entry into the waves; others shook free, rolled clear, and were beginning to claw their way shoreward.

'They're bloody late,' Turk snarled, and turned with binoculars raised.

The first six or seven infantry assault craft had achieved the shallows and were beaching a hundred yards short of the Bernières sea-wall, but a mile and a half westward both tanks and swarming troops were already ashore, with several major landing craft grounded and disembarking armour and guns. To eastward was another congestion of shipping, which must have been the van of Force S, crowding the shore-line, and overhead, repeatedly, medium bombers and fighter bombers appeared from seaward, flying fast and low through a scurry of enemy tracer. Only here, below Bernières, was a landing being spearheaded by unsupported infantry. There should be tanks ashore by now — gun tanks, flail tanks, flame-throwing tanks — but there was none. The men from the assault craft were scrambling through the surf like ants spreading across the rocks and sand. A second wave of assault craft had joined the first, with the boats jostling for openings and ramps down. There were men down, dozens of them, as machine-gun fire scythed, sprawling in the mud and floating against the wire. A shell burst full among one advancing, crouching group — then a second — scattering sand, stones and twisting bodies.

Four hundred yards and closing.

'Ludd!' Turk shouted. 'Tell the flotilla: "I am about to engage to starboard. Follow me."' He cupped his mouth with his hands to bawl at the fore-deck below. 'Bunter! Stand by starboard battery. We are running in close and turning to port. For God's sake be careful of the soldiers.'

There was a new burst of noise, a sudden clatter that resembled a handful of pebbles being thrown viciously into a tin bath. Bullets sputtered against the ship's side, ripped through the splinter mats around the Lewis guns and sheared fist-sized holes in the thin metal of the funnel.

'Shave off,' Perk exclaimed. 'Them's real bullets.'

ERA Gilbert lowered himself hastily into the engine-room, slamming the hatch above him, and, in the forward mess-deck, SBA Peach stretched himself on the deck between the tables.

*

The time-table for Juno, the centre of the three British sectors, had been disrupted by the weather. The infantry assault craft had reached the beach half an hour late, and the German guncrews, little harmed by the pre-assault bombardment which had been over-ranged, were warned, waiting and ready. Worse, the 8th Canadian Brigade reached the beach below Bernières and St Aubin ahead of the amphibious tanks that should have preceded them.

The little wooden LCAs, each with a naval crew of four and embarking thirty-five troops crouched below the gunwhale, grounded in the rocky shallows, some of them swinging broadside as the following tide took their sterns. The infantrymen had experienced twenty-four hours of misery before descending the wet, swaying scrambling-nets from the landing ships into the bucketing LCAs, and that final hour, between ship and beach, had been the worst of their lives. Confined and nauseated, they had seen nothing but a sky above that swirled with smoke, heard nothing except an engine roar and the crump-crump of gunfire. Then there were shouts and the bow ramp had crashed open. They had spilled out into several feet of water floating with debris, holding their weapons high, seeing the beach, the sea-wall and the houses beyond for the first time.

Men were being smashed down immediately, even before they waded free of the water, by enemy fire from several directions not easy to identify, but dominating the foreshore was a massive concrete bunker that vomited cannon-fire, and a knot of assault craft had inadvertently beached immediately before it. Fortuitously, the lateness of the landing had meant that a fuller tide had carried the craft high up the beach; the sanctuary of the sea-wall was a mere hundred yards away. To reach it, however, was impossible. The men went to ground, momentarily protected by a climbing bank of shingle, but unable to advance or retire. A few sheltered behind the assault craft as bullets lashed into the sea around them. Bodies floated in the red-scummed water, tumbling grotesquely in the tide's movement.

The respite, however, could only be brief. The several companies of Canadians, pinned down and with only light weapons, would soon be sought out by mortars or blasted by high-explosive shells. A few men crawled forward in an attempt to get within grenade-throwing range, but the enemy's well-sited guns quickly flung them headlong.

Then, with a thunderous roar, the big concrete bastion with its lethal gun-slits suddenly disappeared behind a colossal eruption of shale, sand and smoke. The shaken, prone infantrymen clawed at the earth as a torrent of shell-fire poured from seaward, only feet above them, obliterating the face of the bunker, smashing into the walls, sandbags and steelwork. The noise was deafening, the dust choking in their throats, and, trapped between the enemy and the devastating barrage from the rear, they cringed unmoving.

Only yards off-shore, so audaciously close that it seemed incredible she did not run aground, the LCF rolled in a pall of gun-smoke, her entire starboard battery of two-pounders and Oerlikons pounding, aflame, and her great ensign curling and flapping in the wind. The range at which her gun-crews fired was so short that it was almost impossible to miss, but only fractionally below the line of sight were the hundreds of Canadian infantrymen clinging to cover under the long swell of shingle, and the smallest error, the briefest moment of carelessness, would be tragically fatal. Astern of LCF49, half a cable distant and just turning, followed another LCF, and then a third, pouring thousands of shells at the sea-wall and its gun embrasures, the houses beyond the promenade road.

'Pick the bones o' that, yer bastards,' Perk exulted, and turned to Walt. 'I got through three bleedin' magazines. I must 'ave killed about four 'undred.'

'Ours or theirs?' Walt asked.

*

The enemy strong-points along the beach and sea-wall between Bernières and St Aubin were blackened shells or piles of rubble, smashed by the LCFs' barrage, and the only resistance came from isolated snipers who were being prised from their hiding-places by the Canadians with grenades. The first of the DD tanks was crawling ashore, a second wave of LCAs with the Regiment de la Chaudiere, then LCTs with more tanks, engineer assault vehicles and light artillery. 'From Group Commander, sir,' Lobby Ludd reported. '"Well done".'

Turk nodded. 'Bunter, it's a bloody good job your Marines had some practice since they tried to shoot down that drogue off Ardrossan, or we might have had congratulations from Rommel.'

The flotilla had turned westward, in line ahead, clear of the rock-studded shallows. In every ship fresh boxes of ammunition were being hurriedly hoisted from the magazine, the guns reloaded and expended shell-cases cleared away. The cluttered houses of Courseulles lay to port, behind another beach now thickly thronged with assault craft, many capsized and wrecked, but with the foreshore choked with armoured vehicles, trucks and guns. A foothold, albeit tenuous, had been achieved, and fighting had moved from the beach area into the streets beyond. From five hundred yards off-shore could still be heard the rumble of gunfire, and there were black puff-balls in the overcast sky inland, climbing columns of smoke. The flotilla steamed parallel to the shore-line, looking for targets but seeing none, then turned back to reconnoitre the eastern extremity of the Juno sector where it bordered on that of Sword — several miles of shore-line across which the neighbouring assault groups had not yet deployed.

The heavier vessels of the invasion fleet were closing — more LSTs, infantry ships, the hospital carrier St Juliett, and scores of smaller craft waiting to unload but prevented from doing so because of increasing congestion ashore. The beaches were becoming crowded with vehicles unable to disperse quickly by the few mine-cleared exits and the narrow, equally crowded roads behind. From somewhere inland an enemy 88-mm battery had opened fire, finding its range with uncanny accuracy.

'Either they're ranging on the barrage balloons,' Turk said, 'or they've got an observation post with a clear view of the beachhead.'

Binoculars searched the shore, but an artillery observer with a small radio or field telephone could be hidden almost anywhere. The salvoes of shells from the distant battery were falling among the clogged and frustrated lines of vehicles which, every minute, were being joined by still more from the disembarking ships. A confusion was threatening that could turn the already delayed landing into a debacle.

'They're cutting the balloons adrift,' Summers noted.

Perk suggested that, if only somebody had said, he would have shot them down. 'If yer ain't going ter use them full magazines, Walt,' he offered, feeling superior, 'I'll 'ave them over 'ere.' Walt, on the port side, had not yet enjoyed an opportunity for firing his Lewis guns.

Lobby Ludd had a telescope on the headquarters ship, Hilary, from which a lamp was blinking, difficult to read through smoke and the masts of other vessels. ERA Gilbert's head and shoulders had reappeared above the engine-hatch.

Three more shells, in quick succession, burst over the crowded beach. Turk whirled. 'There's only one place with a clear sighting — '

'From Hilary, sir,' Lobby Ludd yelled. '"Immediate Engage Dogfish repeat Dogfish."'

Turk and Summers raced to the chart table. 'I thought so,' Turk snorted. 'Bunter, here's something you've wanted to do all your life.' He pointed. 'Knock down that chimney.'

Just to the westward and behind Courseulles the chimney reared, smokeless, two hundred feet above the nearest houses, and its summit easily overlooked the beach area for several miles in each direction. If there was an access ladder there was no sign of it from seaward, and there was no evidence of occupancy, but it would have required little ingenuity to hide an observation point inside its upper parapet.

'Port battery,' Turk ordered. 'We'll get as near as we can. Start when you're ready, Bunter. If you concentrate your fire about half-way up, it ought to topple — but cease fire immediately it starts. Our own troops can't be spitting distance away. No, Walters, don't bother with those Lewis guns.'

'Sir,' Walt pleaded, 'I'm loaded an' cocked — '

'All right. But don't blaze away at the wild blue yonder, like Hot-Shot Perkins on the starboard side. We're only fighting a war, not making a bloody John Wayne film.'

At a range of four hundred yards the six guns of the port battery opened fire, flinging their ribbons of tracer smoke over the cluttered roofs of the shore houses towards the tall pencil of the chimney. Within seconds the two-pounder shells were smashing into the target. The splinter of brickwork was clearly visible before being obscured by billowing dust that rose skyward.

'Cease fire,' Turk shouted. The guns stopped hammering and the distant dust-cloud dispersed. Frustratingly, the chimney still stood, holed but erect. Turk swore. 'What the hell are you firing, Bunter? Bloody corned beef fritters?'

There was a sudden, brief burst of Lewis gun fire from abaft the bridge, and Turk, Summers and Lobby Ludd ducked below the screen. Four hundred yards away the massive chimney shuddered, broke into segments, and collapsed slowly into an explosive welter of debris.

'Shave off,' Walt marvelled. 'Sorry I didn't do it the first time, sir. I got jammed.' He sniffed. 'If there's anything else yer'd like knocked down — '

*

ERA Gilbert had climbed to the bridge, wiping oily hands on cotton waste and eyeing the smoke-hazed shore warily.

'That last skylark, sir,' he reported, 'did us a bit o' no good. We must 'ave hit a rock.' He shrugged. 'I don't know what we did ter the rock, but the port screw ain't what she used ter be. Either it's lost a blade or it's fouling the rudder shaft. Anyway, we ain't going nowhere very fast, sir. I've shut down the port engine.'

Turk grimaced, heaved a breath, and rubbed an unshaven chin. 'That's all we needed.' He nodded. 'All right Number One, we'll find ourselves a nice stretch of private beach, run ashore, and dry out.'

'You mean' — Summers was uncertain — 'ashore here — now, sir? But we won't be able to kedge off until tonight.'

'I can't think of another way of looking at our screws,' Turk said. 'Anyway, I fancy we could all stretch our legs.'

Six

LCF49 ran ashore under the sea-wall of Courseulles, among men of the Regina Regiment who were still dragging corpses from the tangled wreckage of small craft in the shallows. There was a litter of abandoned equipment, crushed into the shingle by tank tracks — weapons, webbing and water-bottles, helmets, a boot that still contained a severed foot, spent cartridges, broken sandbags collapsed over empty gun-pits. 'It's like Southend, the day after Bank 'Oliday,' Lobby Ludd decided. 'There's even blokes queuing fer the Mystery Trip.' A long file of German prisoners, sullen-faced, waited to be embarked in a tank landing craft.

As soon as the tide had receded the damage to the ship was apparent. The port rudder had obviously struck an underwater obstacle, either rock or concrete, and its steel shaft had been wrenched to just foul the screw. Miraculously, the only damage to the screw was a small, V-shaped cleft, the size of a fingernail, in the tip of each blade. If the rudder shaft could be straightened, the screw's function would seem to be unimpaired. The distorted shaft, however, was twice the thickness of a man's arm, and the possibility of achieving repairs on an open beach still within range of enemy guns, a battleline only a mile away and a German counter-attack likely at any moment, was remote. The group of men on the cluttered, wet sand under the stern eyed the damaged rudder dejectedly.

'Somewhere around here,' Turk said, 'there's a dock-and-repair ship, but I don't know where. If we show up with this, we might find ourselves ordered back to Southampton. Even worse, we could be told to unship the guns and scuttle her in deep water. There's not going to be much employment for close support craft once the landing's established, and it might be thought that a dry-docking for repairs just can't be justified — not for two or three weeks of operational life. We could be written off,' he snorted, 'and all because of a bloody bent pintle.'

They stared at him, mildly shocked, not having seen their predicament in such a serious light. 'I suppose we couldn't saw it off, and pretend we didn't know?' Taplow chuckled, but nobody smiled.

Lobby Ludd had descended to the sand from the bridge. 'From Group Commander, sir. "Report state of seaworthiness immediately,"' Turk frowned.

'Sir,' Lobby Ludd suggested, 'if it was bent crooked, it can be bent straight, can't it?' He pointed. 'Them Canadians up the beach 'ave got a soddin' great bulldozer that's pushing around clapped-out tanks like they was nothing. I reckon if yer gave the bloke a couple o' tots — '

Turk stared in the direction indicated. 'Summers,' he said slowly, 'why didn't it occur to you that a ship could be repaired by a bloody bulldozer? Because it sounds damn stupid. That's why the Admiralty still says that tanks won't float.' He grinned. 'Ludd, if Group Commander flashes again, it'll be impossible for you to read him through the smoke, and tell Henry that his VHF receiver has developed a fault. It'll take him half an hour to fix it. Number One, lets you and me take a stroll up the beach.'

A Canadian major was momentarily doubtful about halting the pressing task of clearing the beach approaches of the dozens of foundered tanks and trucks that were delaying the invasion of Europe, but the mention of a bottle of Scotch modified his philosophy. There were such things as priorities and, after all, the navy was the senior service. Who was he to argue? The massive bulldozer, belching exhaust fumes, throttled a passage over the debris-strewn shingle and aligned itself below the ship's stern. Turk was on hands and knees as the monster jockeyed for position above him, then raised a thumb. With a loud roar the bulldozer lurched forward, hesitated as its ram met the solid steel of the rudder shaft, but shuddered on. The shaft strained for seconds, then yielded as if made of wax. Turk scrambled clear.

'It's not exactly a precision job,' he told everyone, 'but we're back in business. Nobody's going to believe it.' He brushed wet sand from his knees. 'Ludd, you can tell Group Commander: "Minor repairs completed. Will kedge off at next tide." And Henry has fixed the fault in his receiver. Number One, the off-duty hands can go ashore, so long as they don't roam too far and are back aboard by fifteen hundred. Tell Perkins and Walters that the army doesn't need their help to take Bayeux. Ah, yes, Ludd, when we get back to Southampton, Mrs Ludd can come aboard any time she likes.'

*

When LCF49 had beached earlier there had been an American-built but British-manned tank landing craft rolling, waterlogged, in the surf, having sustained severe damage during the first landing. The surviving half-dozen crewmen, trapped in their craft, had retreated to the only armoured position, the wheel-house, where the glass of the big compass bowl had been broken by concussion. Everything American had to be bigger than non-American counterparts. The compass was filled with pure alcohol, and the crewmen decided that, if they were going to die, they would do so gloriously. When help did arrive they were all happily comatose.

The men from LCF49 climbed from the beach in a group. 'What did he mean, "Mrs Ludd can come aboard any bleedin' time she likes?"' Lobby Ludd asked. 'What's Mrs Ludd got ter do with a soddin' bent rudder bracket?'

Courseulles seemed deserted by civilians, and there were splintered walls, rubble, doors and windows smashed. Tanks, guns and amphibious carriers choked with soldiers churned past in an endless convoy towards the noise of battle, southward, and walking in the narrow street was hazardous. They found an untended, wrecked bar in which every bottle left by earlier explorers was smashed, the floor scattered with broken glass, plaster, upturned chairs and a cranky, upright piano. 'Not a bleedin' aperitif in sight,' Perk said disgustedly. 'There ain't even water in the tap.'

Walt had appropriated a German light machine-gun from an abandoned gun-pit, complete with a fifty-round magazine, and was experimenting with its mechanism, to the apprehension of his fellows, who avoided being in line with the muzzle despite Walt's assurances that he knew exactly what he was doing. 'So did soddin' Al Capone,' Perk nodded. Then, in a dark corner, ERA Gilbert found a barrel which, on being kicked, sounded interestingly full.

Walt offered to shoot a hole in it, but there was no difficulty in extracting the bung. The barrel expended a pale golden liquid, slightly effervescent, which tasted suspiciously like cider, but which ERA Gilbert, on rolling it around his tongue, declared was draught champagne, although not an outstanding vintage. Speculation however, was academic, and there were thirty gallons of it. It was agreed that, since the barrel could not be rolled back to the ship, nor could it be left to be drunk by soldiers who had serious business awaiting them up the road, there remained only one course of action.

There was a miscellany of glasses, still intact, under the bar, and they selected the largest. With thirty gallons, large glasses were necessary, or they might not empty the barrel before 1500. Stoker Bowles investigated the potential of the piano, but his rendering of a dirge about an emasculated Samuel Hall was unable to compete with the roar of tanks and trucks passing within a few feet of the door. SBA Peach complained that he had always been allergic to draught champagne and was beginning to feel sick. He had known it from the start.

'There's people like the Aga Khan', said ERA Gilbert, refilling his flower-vase, 'that pay 'undreds of pounds ter come ter France and drink champagne. Thousands, even.'

SBA Peach decided to explore the upper floor by means of the broken stairs, but in the first room he entered there lay a dead German soldier with half a head and no hands. Peach regained the bar hurriedly, searching for the sink, just as the military policeman entered from the noisy street.

He was immaculate, with polished boots and gleaming brass, a thin face with a sandy moustache under a helmet marked with a red band and letters 'MP', and he regarded the sailors with an icy stare. 'Looting in wartime,' he pronounced, 'is a serious offence. If you ain't out of 'ere before I count five, there's going ter be trouble.'

Nobody appeared concerned. 'What yer supposed ter say, mate,' Lobby Ludd advised, 'is, "'Ello,'ello,'ello. What's all this then?" — then bounce up 'an down on yer toes. Count up ter five, did yer say? Shave off.' He sniffed. 'It's a good job yer've got bleedin' fingers. Now — push off, there's a good little pongo. We're on shore leave.'

The MP paled damply and sucked his teeth. Then he drew a deep breath. 'I'll tell yer just once more,' he gritted. 'Clear this bar — now — or I'm placing yer all under arrest, charged with looting an' drunken insubordination — ' Nobody appeared very concerned. ERA Gilbert refilled his flower-vase and Stoker Bowles launched into '"'Ave yer ever caught yer bollocks in a rat-trap?"' SBA Peach shuddered.

'Yer all under arrest,' the MP shouted. 'Git fell in outside.' Nobody appeared concerned. 'Matey,' Perk offered patiently, 'if I was you, I'd shove off, smartish. If yer don't, yer could get yer lamps trimmed.' He waved a hand in the direction of Peach. 'D'yer see Punch-drunk Peach there?' Peach's head was lowered over the bar sink. 'Peachey's the welterweight champion o' the Home Fleet. Yer should 'ave seen what he did ter Len Harvey. He was never the same bleedin' man after three rounds wi' Peachey. He's a killer when he's roused.'

Peach lifted a white, drawn face.

'Don't think that because you're navy,' the MP snarled, 'you ain't subject to military law.' He fingered the flap of his holster. 'I don't want ter draw my gun.'

Walt suddenly emitted a satisfied yelp. 'I've got it. It's the soddin' trigger,' he told everyone, and cocked his machine-gun. 'They're bleedin' clever, these Germans. If yer press this bit, yer get single shots, see, but if yer want ter fire a burst — ' He squinted along the sights.

ERA Gilbert rapped the liquor barrel with his knuckles. 'We ain't drunk half yet.' He glanced up. 'What's 'appened ter that pongo? He's gone. I suppose it was Peachey again, turnin' nasty.' He refilled his flower-vase and swallowed on a belch. 'Bowlesey, 'ow about singing "Temptation"?'

'I will now sing "Temptation",' announced Stoker Bowles. 'There's a bloke upstairs,' SBA Peach gasped, 'with no 'ands.'

Perk nodded. 'That comes from biting yer nails, or abusing yerself. Or yer can go blind.'

*

The incoming tide swirled around the hull. A hundred feet astern, the grounded kedge on which LCF49 would winch herself off the beach had already disappeared under the waves. Lieutenant Turk paced the bridge impatiently. 'Who's still adrift, Number One?'

'Well, not adrift yet, sir. There's still a few minutes to go. It's Ludd, Gilbert, Perkins, Walters, Bowles and Peach — the usual crowd. We can't start main engines, and I'll need the seamen aft when we kedge off — '

'Damn and bugger it,' Turk snorted. 'I should have known better than to turn that lot loose. It's supposed to be an invasion, not a glorious booze-up.'

Summers had his binoculars on the sea-wall. 'Here they come, sir.' He sighed. 'Walters has a machine-gun, and Gilbert seems to be wearing a flower-vase instead of his hat. Ludd and Perkins are carrying Peach, and I think Bowles is just singing into an imaginary microphone.'

'If there was just one bloody bar in twenty miles, they'll have found it,' Turk said. 'Get 'em aboard, Number One, and get Gilbert into the engine-room. Then stand by to heave up to the kedge.'

Minutes later the kedge-hawser was straining and the screws churned in a brown froth as the ship eased herself, stern first, from the beach. A hundred yards clear Summers reported, 'All secured, sir.'

'Number One,' Turk frowned, 'there's a jeep roaring along the beach, with an officer and three military policemen shouting and waving. It looks like they're shouting at us.'

Summers raised his binoculars. 'Perhaps they're just shouting goodbye and good luck, sir. Unless, of course, they heard about the bulldozer and the bottle of Scotch.'

'No,' Turk decided, 'I don't think it's that.' He glanced at his watch. 'Just wave back, Number One, and smile. Then let's get to hell out of here. If anyone asks, we never came to Courseulles, and if we did, nobody went ashore — and get rid of that bloody German machine-gun. I fancy we nearly had six of our crew in military custody for aiding and abetting the enemy.'

*

'Under cover of darkness LCF49 will occupy the position vacated by Warspite.'

There seemed no sense in it until later. During the entire day there had been no sign of enemy aircraft over the landing areas, and information on the progress of the troops ashore percolated only slowly to the crowded ships off-shore. That five beachheads had been established they well knew, but were aware of little more. The noise and smoke of battle were still apparent beyond the rise of the shore-line. They did not know that none of the hoped-for D-Day objectives had been achieved, that the American Utah landing was isolated, and Omaha was still separated by seven miles from Gold. The latter had linked with Juno, but there remained a gap of three miles between Juno and Sword. Because of the bad sea conditions, and not helped by the congestion on the beaches, the disembarkation of reinforcements and supplies was eight hours behind the desired schedule. Then, with darkness, Heinkels of the Luftwaffe broke free of the grip of the RAF and screamed low over Juno.

The whine of aircraft engines and the crump-crump of bombs were audible for a full minute before the broadcast Red Alert sent gun-crews scrambling to their stations. The attackers were invisible, but a barrage of criss-crossing tracer from a hundred ships filled the sky, and it seemed incredible that any aircraft could have survived for seconds. The fourteen guns of LCF49 flung thousands of shells into the darkness overhead, and had just ceased firing, confident that the hit-and-run attack was over, when a howling roar of twin engines passed so close above the mast-head that everyone crouched involuntarily.

'Those other aircraft were a feint!' Turk shouted. 'They're after Warspite!'

'Soddin' marvellous,' Perk said. 'And I'm bleedin' standing exactly where Warspite's quarterdeck oughter be.'

It made sense now — that earlier the position of the anchored battleship had been pin-pointed by the enemy, and the British had anticipated it. Warspite had been moved out of danger, substituted for by a much smaller, expendable vessel, but whose intensive volume of anti-aircraft fire would convince enemy pilots, flying in darkness and partially confused by flak, that the battleship still lay below.

To port the sea erupted. Four massive water-spouts rose, whitely, clearly visible. A fifth and sixth lifted the sea just astern. The LCF rolled to starboard as if flinching from a blow, and salt rained over the crouched gun-crews. A glass insulator at the mast-head splintered and the aerial fell, snaking over bridge and fore-deck. The ship lurched back to port, with the Marines clawing at their guns, but it was too late. The roar of engines was fading as the enemy fled into the night, just above sea level.

'From Group Commander on VHF, sir,' Lobby Ludd reported. '"Are you all right? I bet the Luftwaffe will be disappointed. Haw-Haw won't be able to ask quote Where is the Warspite? unquote."'

'I bet I wasn't disappointed,' Walt sniffed. 'I nearly asked quote Where is bleedin' LCF49 unquote.'

The early objectives, St Lo and Caen, had not yet been captured, but the enemy's armoured counter-attack had been beaten off and only the westward Utah beachhead was not linked with its fellows. However, the slowness in disembarking stores, particularly ammunition, was causing increasing concern. The first huge components of Mulberries 'A' and 'B', the prefabricated concrete harbours, were being settled into position off St Laurent and Arromanches, while a sad collection of old ships was being scuttled off-shore to provide a sheltering wall for unloading vessels. They included the dirty, pre-1914 French battleship Courbet, which had stagnated in Portsmouth since 1940, the equally old British Centurion, since 1924 employed as a target ship and more recently as a dummy King George V battleship, the Netherlands cruiser Sumatra, and the D-class cruiser Durban — the latter to be joined by her sister ship, the Polish-manned Dragony after she had been torpedoed earlier in the operation.

Even so, disembarkation was excruciatingly slow. And at any moment, it was anticipated, Grand-Admiral Doenitz would launch his seaborne offensive — his new electro-U-boats, E-boats, midget submarines, human torpedoes and circling torpedoes — which if unleashed among the crowded ships along the Normandy coast, could inflict crippling damage.

There had to be a protective screen around the beach-head to seaward. There had to be a Trout Line.

With the approach of every evening the LCFs and LCGs lifted anchor and filed quietly out of the clutter of shipping, northward, into the open Channel until the shore-line disappeared astern, then anchored again, two cables apart in a long, curving cordon — the Trout Line — that included small armed vessels of every category. Many, like the MLs, mounted only a single three-pounder and a pair of .303 machine-guns, while MTBs had torpedo tubes that were irrelevant. Depth charges were made up from half a dozen sticks of explosive bundled together with a fuse and detonator, activated by stamping under the heel of a boot and then flung over the side. Smoke could be made by means of smoke canisters — dustbin-sized containers, again activated by a hammer blow against a nose-cap, and which would float if jettisoned. The canisters were stowed in bows and stern, and when the situation demanded, one or the other would be fired in accordance with wind direction — so that the smoke flowed away from the ship. A change of wind direction or, more likely, an error in calculation, that sent the smoke over the ship could be disastrous. The thick, black, asphyxiating smoke flooded every deck and every cranny, prostrating vomiting crewmen, and a fighting vessel could be incapacitated in seconds.

All ships were darkened, with engines stopped, and the men at their stations on bridge and fore-deck waited in silence, listened for noises other than the sea's whisper and the sigh of the wind in the halyards, watched the dark surrounding void for the green glimmer of phosphorescence that could betray the passage of a half-submerged enemy or could, more usually, mean nothing. Sometimes there would be a muttered warning and they would strain their ears, hearing the far distant throb of slow-running engines, and the guns would turn their muzzles quietly, tracking, all praying for a glimpse of an approaching shape blacker than the horizon sky to northward. Then, suddenly, the distant throb would explode into a roar as the probing enemy sensed the waiting net and flung himself about, desperately seeking the safety of distance and darkness. The guns would crash, the muzzles flashing with brilliant yellow that dazed the eyes and starkly silhouetted the crews tensed over their sights, then as quickly fall silent with the enemy fled beyond reach. There would be nothing again, except the whisper of the sea and the gently humming wind, and they would shift their weight from one leg to the other, listening, craving the solace of tobacco, tired and chilled, but knowing the night had long to go, and there were no reliefs on the Trout Line; it was an all night trick.

And the nights were either full of incidents, of alarms, gunfire, shouts of warning over VHF, tracer in the blackness, as the enemy probed and probed but never penetrated — or there was nothing. It was difficult to decide which was the more fatiguing. At dawn LCF49 raised her kedge, steamed slowly along the tethered line of fellows as they hauled in. LCF1, with her two twin turrets, would follow astern, then LCF19, LCF20, LCF24, LCF31, the ungainly LCGs, and the long procession, in line ahead, would file back into the vast anchorage of ships, almost unnoticed as others, awakening, cooked their breakfasts, to reanchor, to sling hammocks and sleep like men comatose, unwashed, unshaven, and caring nothing.

The men of the Trout Line had heard of, but knew little about, midget submarines and human torpedoes. In December 1941 the Italians had disabled the battleships Valiant and Queen Elizabeth in Alexandria harbour, employing Maiale craft, two-man submergible 'chariots' carrying detachable warheads with delayed detonators. Both Germans and Japanese were known to have midget submarines, and British 'X' craft had attacked Tirpitz in Alten fjord; but descriptions were vague. It was generally assumed, however, that none had the endurance, seaworthiness or speed to operate effectively in open sea conditions, and nobody had heard of the German Neger one-man torpedo-submarine.

The Neger, in essence, comprised two torpedo bodies, one conventional and suspended from the other, in which the single crewman sat, occupying a cockpit enclosed by a perspex dome. Unlike the earlier 'chariots', from which the explosive warhead had to be manually detached and clamped to the hull of an enemy vessel, the Neger required only to be steered within range, aimed and the lower torpedo discharged.

German training with this and other new weapons, however, had been brief, production had been rushed, and the Neger was temperamental in performance. When the lower, missile torpedo was released, the sudden loss of trim was such that only expert handling on the part of the crewman prevented his craft from surfacing violently. It was an eccentricity which, given time, would doubtless have been corrected, but Doenitz had no more time.

No U-boats had yet evaded the Channel patrols, whose attention was also unlikely to be avoided by surface vessels larger than E-boats, coast-hugging by night. The Trout Line was a match for E-boats so long as they were not allowed to sneak between two anchored craft in the darkness. If that happened, the Germans would enjoy a measure of immunity because the cross-fire from the British ships was as likely to endanger friend as foe.

There were also reports of an explosive motor-boat which could be directed at a target before the single crewman jumped overboard, and circling torpedoes which, if released among the packed ships in the anchorage, could not fail to find a victim. Nobody was sure if these reports were factual or speculative.

*

LCF49 winched in her kedge at dawn, as she had on a dozen previous dawns. It was going to be a chill, blustery day. The grey sea slap-slapped against the side as Sub-Lieutenant Summers peered over the stern, then turned to raise an arm to indicate that the cable was vertical and the kedge free of the bottom. In the wheel-house the telegraphs clanged. A trickle of smoke rose from the galley chimney, and Lobby Ludd hoisted the ship's pennants. Lieutenant Bunter climbed to the bridge to join Turk in listening to the day's first BBC news bulletin. In twenty minutes the ship and her following flotilla would be anchored again, inshore, and the gun-crews thought of breakfast, their waiting hammocks, and uninterrupted sleep until noon. This was the moment when, the long night finished, men surrendered to their consuming fatigue. They yawned, stretched, and turned their thoughts away from the sea and sky they had watched for hours. It was the moment of dulled perception, the moment of peril.

'This is the BBC Forces Programme. Here is the six o'clock news, and this is Alvar Liddell reading it ... '

Lobby Ludd lit a cigarette. His mouth was rancid and he looked, he guessed, as slovenly as he felt. Lieutenant Turk had a weary elbow on the wheel-house voice-pipe. Both gazed abstractedly at the ship being overtaken to starboard, LCF1, now separated from them by only forty yards of sullen water but not yet under way. Turk could see the cable party on her after-deck, hosing the mud from the kedge as it emerged from the sea — three seamen and the First Lieutenant. They would be cold-fingered and anxious to be finished. There were two figures on the bridge, and one of them waved. Turk lifted a hand in return. In a few seconds LCF49 would be ahead, and the other, with screws in motion, would follow astern — then LCF19, and LCF20 ...

When they secured again, Lobby Ludd was thinking, there might be some mail. It was time they had some soddin' mail. And he hoped that somebody on the mess-deck was wetting the tea, and hadn't forgotten there were still blokes on bleedin' watch. Likely there'd be a letter from Mrs Ludd, to tell him that tinned snoek was like salmon, only different, and give her love to the sailors downstairs. He never understood that bit. And there'd be a letter from Freda Harris saying what a good thing it was that they had not arranged anything for June, with all this invasion thing. Did he know anyone who had gone to it?

'During the night and the early hours of this morning the RAF and the Ninth US Air Force attacked rail installations and flying bomb launching sites in northern France and Belgium. Fierce fighting has been continuing around Caen and St Lo ... ' To starboard there was a massive, shattering explosion — a thunderclap that tortured the ears and terrified the senses. Turk shouted. Seconds later a searing shockwave struck the ship broadside and the deck tilted. Turk, Bunter and Lobby Ludd clawed for hand-holds, bewildered, but beyond the screen a horrendous pall of yellow smoke reared hundreds of feet skyward, higher and higher, spilling outward like an immense, leprous mushroom. Beneath it LCF1 had disappeared. 'My God,' Turk choked, 'she's gone.' It was impossible. Only a moment before, less than fifty yards from them, a ship of 540 tons and 160 feet long had lain solidly in the water, with men working on deck and a waved greeting from the bridge — and now it had gone as quickly as a bursting soap bubble. It was impossible.

And in another moment all three men flung themselves to the deck as the sky rained debris — twisted steel, cork rafts, oil drums, mess-stools, a splintered dinghy, and unidentifiable, spinning shapes that could have been anything, all smashing into a churning, clay-coloured sea that floated with sodden refuse and burning cordite.

'Christ!' Turk's face was incredulous. 'What was it?'

Lobby Ludd hauled himself upright. The action bell was hammering, and on deck men were struggling into their gun harnesses as others scrambled from below. Lieutenant Taplow, jacketless and hatless, kicked at the clips of the magazine hatch that only minutes before had been secured. Gun muzzles weaved, uncertain. There was nothing to be seen to starboard except a sea of filth floating with glowing cordite that spat and smoked, a few corpses with oddly yellow faces lifted to the sky, a single survivor clinging to a smoke canister …

'There it is!' Lobby Ludd bawled, pointing. 'On the port side! The port side!' There was a well-drilled formula for reporting an enemy vessel — identity, relative bearing, distance and, if possible, course and speed — but there were moments when a pointing finger had to suffice. He could not understand why no other sod could see. 'Fer Chrissake — the port side!'

Others now, however, were seeing. A dull grey, slim cylindrical shape, on a course almost identical to that of the ship, had broken surface, rearing from a shallow trough so close to the side that the midships guns would have difficulty in depressing sufficiently to engage. Clearly visible was the craft's transparent cockpit cover and, within, the head and shoulders of its crewman with face turned. The blunt nose of the cylinder, resembling a torpedo with a blister on its upper side, lifted higher, fell clumsily as a wave broke over it, then turned away from the LCF as every gun of the port battery was being wrenched in its direction.

The German's tactic was fatal. Had he turned towards his enemy and, assuming he still retained his diving capability, plunged under the LCF's hull, he might have survived, but now, seeking distance, he had done the one thing that assured his destruction. The crews of two two-pounders and four Oerlikons fastened their sights on the target, barely the length of a cricket pitch away, and pressed their triggers. Lieutenant Bunter, to Walt's disgust, had reached the port twin Lewis guns first. Hundreds of shells smashed into the fleeing torpedo craft, boiling the sea and raking the target to shreds like wet paper under a spiked boot. Every gunner kept finger on trigger until every shell in every magazine had gone, then snarled for another. Turk shouted for cease fire, but nobody heard. There was a rage in every man that had to be consumed, and the last gun fell silent only when all trace of the enemy torpedo-submarine and its crewman had been obliterated from the sea's surface.

They hauled the single survivor aboard. He was a young able seaman, stupefied with shock, his hands so tightly clenched on the casing of the smoke canister that two men were lowered into the sea to prise loose his fingers and lift him to the deck. His face was expressionless, eyes blank, as Peach rubbed him, wrapped him in heated blankets and fed him a measure of brandy from the wardroom cabinet.

Then, when comprehension returned, he talked and talked, the words tumbling from his lips in a nervous, unceasing stream. He had been hosing the kedge as the winch hauled in, he told them several times, leaning over the stern, and it was bleedin' cold. Then the deck had lifted under his feet and, amazed, he saw the kedge fall back into the sea from which it had just climbed. Almost simultaneously a monstrous blast, like the blow of a massive fist, had struck him from behind, and he was blind and deaf, without form or sense, place or knowing — except he knew he was dead. He wondered if Knocker White was dead, because Knocker was his brother-in-law, having married his sister only last month. Christ only knew what Marlene was going to bleedin' say after this. Then two blokes were pulling him from the smoke canister, and he had lost four of his front teeth. Christ. He'd only been standing there, hosing the mud off the kedge ...

*

On several occasions, during daytime, the men had scrambled frantically to their guns at the throaty chutter of a VI flying bomb overhead, heading to seaward and the English coast, but warning was always too brief and the missiles invariably too fast and too high to be caught by anti-aircraft fire, and they watched frustrated as the detested winged bombs vanished over the horizon. The battle for France was moving further inland, but the supply situation remained on a razor's edge. Three days and nights of vicious gales drove convoys back to port, spread chaos among the ships unloading over open beaches, tore to pieces the American Mulberry harbour off St Laurent, and stranded eight hundred invaluable landing craft. To the little ships of the Trout Line they were days and nights of numbing exhaustion, of dragging anchors, wet clothes and cold food, a howling wind and a constantly battering sea from which there was never a moment's respite. Ships like these had not been designed to ride out gales on the open sea, and many were perilously near to foundering. Paradoxically, it was the more experienced seamen, who always boasted that present conditions were never as harrowing as they had been in some previous ship, who were aware just how hazardous the situation was; the less knowing, derided by their betters, were less apprehensive.

And they knew even less about the oyster mines than they had about midget submarines. Acoustic and magnetic mines they knew about; all mines were passively insidious, like the snake under a rock, and they were blindly indiscriminate, but degaussing and intensive sweeping in the Channel had reduced the hazard. The oyster — the pressure mine — was different. It was detonated by the reduction of pressure when a ship passed above it, and it could not be swept. Scores of these had been sown by aircraft, but most of them farther eastward, where the Germans were convinced the main Allied invasion was intended even after the landings in Normandy had been made. The gales of late June, however, had shifted many oysters westward, added to by low-flying German aircraft at night.

*

Perk had gone to the hospital ship to have a tooth extracted, and returned highly amused. The hospital ship had arrived off the beachhead only hours earlier, and Perk had been her first patient. The flashed request from the LCF for an ambulance launch had brought dozens of nurses, orderlies and crew-new to this scene of war or any other — to the rails of the upper deck, expecting to see their first mangled casualties. As the launch came alongside, several orderlies descended the side ladder to help Perk aboard. Two took his shoulders. Take it easy, sailor, they comforted, everything's going to be all right. Someone put a cigarette between his surprised lips and three others tried to light it. A serious-faced Wardmaster, attended by two equally serious Petty Officers, took charge of proceedings, and the onlookers drew back expectantly.

Perk opened his mouth and inserted several fingers. 'Aagh, aagh,' he explained. 'Not the back one — aagh — but the one jes' in front o' the back one.' He drew breath. 'It's been soddin' murder — '

'The nex' minute', he told the mess on his return, 'yer'd think I had bleedin' leprosy.' He had been showing everyone his newly acquired cavity, in which none showed more than distant interest, when LCF31, two stations removed and swinging on her kedge, drifted over the oyster mine.

The explosion broke her back, but her cellular construction served her well, and she was settling only slowly when LCF49 came alongside and secured, bow to bow and bollard to bollard. It was a hazardous stratagem that Turk regretted immediately. The seamen and marines of the stricken ship were clambering to safety, dry-shod, but as the waterlogged vessel sank lower the heavy mooring-ropes that coupled her to LCF 49 had become so tightly clenched on the bollards forward, midships and aft that they could not be thrown off. LCF49's deck tilted ominously, dragged down by her sinking companion, who was already awash.

The last few men were hauled inboard.

'Get rid of those bloody ropes, Number One — fast!' Turk roared.

The deck lurched farther and there was a screech of tortured steel as the flanks of both ships clashed. Aft, Lobby Ludd swung a fire axe desperately, with the deck at such an angle that a foothold was almost impossible. Lieutenant Taplow clutched him around the waist and flung out a hand to be gripped by a panting Marine Gilfedder. Then the heavy coir hawser parted. LCF49 reared like a maddened animal, and an explosive curtain of spray rose thirty feet skyward between the two ships. LCF31, alongside, rolled for the last time, turned over and disappeared as the sea pounced, exulting. Lobby Ludd, Lieutenant Taplow and Marine Gilfedder were flung down in a tangled heap. Gilfedder's iron-shod foot broke Taplow's nose and Gilfedder gashed a knee to the bone, but the ship had shuddered upright, her starboard side battered and scoured to bare metal and every rope lost except the kedge-hawser and the heaving lines.

'Next time we bleedin' tie up, I suppose,' Walt said, 'we'll 'ave ter use Peachey's elastoplast … '

Seven

LCF38 was the next to go, followed by two LCGs and then LCF37. It was, Lobby Ludd suggested, like being ten little nigger boys; at almost every dawn there seemed to be someone missing. And nobody appeared to care much. The BBC news bulletin told of the fall of Cherbourg and the battles around Caen, the flying bombs on London and an extra ration of sugar for jam-making. He had a letter from Freda Harris. Was he really in France? She did not suppose that nylons were easily available, but the French did make super perfumes. There was one called Chanel No. 9, and if he happened to see any ... ?

Mrs Ludd wrote, hoping her letter found him in the pink as it left her, decrying the disappearance of offal from the butcher's, and ending on the news that fares had gone up again and she did not know how anyone could bath decently in four inches.

The Trout Line craft were now being worked to the limits of design capability and the endurance of their crews. The men were fatigued and often dirty; fresh water supplies were not easily available. There was no bread, and they were weary of the hard, emergency biscuits issued as a substitute. All provisions consisted of army K rations — pre-packed cartons, each for twenty men, containing corned beef, soya bean sausages, dried egg, dehydrated potato, tinned pudding, and a khaki-coloured powder which, when added to hot water, resulted in something called tea but which tasted of boiled straw. There were, claimed the issuing authority, three distinct K ration cartons, marked A, B or C, each with different contents, but those that reached the Trout Line for weeks were all marked A. It was all something to do with fooling the enemy, ERA Gilbert said.

'I 'spose someone knows we're still 'ere?' Stoker Bowles asked.

There were rumours of a vast consignment of canned beer being unloaded for the troops ashore, and an ENSA concert party that included women. Just prior to one evening sortie a launch carrying a newsreel cameraman and his assistant came alongside, referred to LCF49 by the Group Commander. Perk raced below to comb his hair, but when he returned to the upper deck the cameraman had gone, following a brief talk with Lieutenant Turk. Regrettably, the shabby Trout Line craft did not have much audience appeal, the news man decided, and, anyway, filming in the dark was never very successful. If he hurried he might be in time to film the ENSA party and a crowd of soldiers with upturned thumbs. A few hours later, just before dawn, LCF49's guns halted the infiltration of an explosive motor-boat, radio-controlled by an E-boat to seaward.

It would have been a major scoop for the news cameraman, but he was sleeping uncomfortably on an air-filled rubber mattress in the back of a five-ton truck in Douvres. He had failed to persuade a leggy blonde tap-dancer from Cardiff to submit to a screen test for a big musical with Michael Wilding. Not in the back of a truck, boyo, she had said. She'd fallen for that one in Aldershot at Christmas, and she was still waiting to hear from Denham Studios.

*

There was a grey sea mist, and the slab-shaped motor-boat lay low in the water fifty yards away, rising and falling sluggishly in the long, flat swell. It appeared to be about ten feet in length, dark-painted, with shell-decked bows and an open, empty cockpit. It had stopped, but whether by accident or intention it was impossible to tell — whether the boat had been immobilized by the earlier flurry of gunfire, its parent E-boat similarly damaged, or the enemy was merely playing possum.

They had watched it for an hour as the light slowly improved. It was like a floating mine that refused to go away, and Turk was reluctant to have his guns destroy it; the capture of an explosive motor-boat, intact, could be useful. The trouble was that he could only guess at its mechanism.

'Probably a torpedo warhead in the bows, with a firing pistol, contact detonated.' But it could be booby-trapped, and two hundred pounds of explosive would make a nasty mess of any amateur attempting to defuse it.

'Radio-controlled steering and throttle — but perhaps a self-destruct device on a time switch.'

There was a wide permutation of possibilities, all of them unpleasant. This nasty little hull and its unpredictable temper were problems for a naval bomb expert, but there was no time. If there was a time-fuse, every passing minute brought an explosion nearer. He wished, now, that he had not waited so long.

He drew a deep breath. 'We're going to defuse it, then take it aboard.' Summers, Bunter and Taplow gazed at him without comment. 'One of us will board it from the dinghy. I haven't the faintest idea how to defuse a bloody explosive motor-boat, and neither do any of you, I suppose — but perhaps that's not a bad thing. Ignorance is bliss. It'll be just a question of disconnecting everything in sight.' He paused. 'And it's got to be an officer, for all sorts of reasons we're not going to discuss now.'

'Instead of trying to defuse it,' Bunter suggested, 'couldn't we tow it on a long line?'

'Tow it where? Into the anchorage? The movement might start something, and it could detonate at any time. The damn thing could be ticking away now. It'd be like dragging a time bomb into a chicken roost.'

'Well, sir — ' Taplow began, but Turk stopped him.

'No, I'm not letting anyone say anything, because I've already decided to do it myself. Nobody would blame us if we just put a few bloody shells into the thing, and then forgot it. That'd be sensible. But because I've chosen the heroic alternative, I'll pull my own chestnuts out of the fire. Number One — '

'Sir — ' Summers interrupted. 'It's different. A ship's captain isn't expected — '

'Balls. Lower the dinghy. There's not much time. I'll need a few tools, and somebody will have to row the dinghy because I can't do two things. When I'm in the motor-boat he can leave me; I shan't do anything until he's well clear. I'd prefer a rating — a volunteer. When I've finished the defusing I'll signal, and you can close on me.'

There was no enthusiasm in his subordinates' faces, but then Lobby Ludd, who had been wiping the glass of the twelve-inch lamp with his cuff, said, 'I'll row yer, sir. I'm Active Service. Everyone else is HOs — except the coxswain and the two sergeants. The coxswain's a married man wi' two sprogs and the sergeants couldn't row a box o' bleedin' dates.' He shrugged. 'HOs are blokes that's in the navy because they got ter be. They ain't entitled ter do these things.'

Turk frowned, then grinned. 'I'm not sure I accept that philosophy, Ludd, but we'll talk about it later. All right. Remember — as soon as I'm in the motor-boat you'll lay off. If you blow up the dinghy you can pay for it.'

The dinghy was swung out and lowered. The mist limited visibility to less than two hundred yards, the decks were wet and there was a pervading dampness that seemed to penetrate the thickest clothing. Summers wanted to wish Turk good luck, but it was too dramatic. He wondered what he should do if his senior killed himself, then decided not to think about it. Everything was so ordinary — Turk and Ludd climbed down into the dinghy, Turk sitting on the stern thwart, Ludd sliding his oars into the rowlocks. If this were a film, Summers thought, there would be stimulating music, close-ups of tense faces and narrowed eyes, and inevitably a heroine in a flimsy nightdress, somewhere, staring at a clock.

Lobby Ludd blew his nose into an immense blue handkerchief and Turk lit a cigarette. Neither man looked up. Walt tossed down the painter.

'I'll put yer breakfus' in the 'eater, Lobby,' he said. 'Yer supposed ter 'ave two eggs on yer plate, mate, but yer've got a soya banger an' red lead.'

A throng of others had gathered around the davits — ERA Gilbert wiping his hands with cotton waste, Perk with the tea kettle, SBA Peach and Telegraphist Henry.

'If this was the bleedin' Serpentine,' Gilbert told Lobby Ludd, 'it'd cost yer 'arf a crown fer a row.'

Lobby Ludd pushed away. It was a laborious row into a swell that rolled strongly towards the hidden French coast, and progress was slow. Several times the drifting motor-boat vanished into a trough, and Turk half-rose, balancing precariously, to keep it in sight. They reached their quarry at last, a black wooden hull shaped like a flat-iron without a handle, ten feet long and with barely twelve inches of freeboard. In darkness it would be invisible. Lobby Ludd, with arms aching, turned the dinghy's stern and leaned on his oars.

'Ah well,' Turk breathed, and sucked his teeth. 'Here goes the last of the Turks.' He swung a leg into the enemy craft. 'I suppose it's too much to expect an instruction manual printed in English. All right, Ludd — push off — and thanks. I'll semaphore if I need anything.'

Lobby Ludd had turned the dinghy around the plunging bows of the motor-boat. 'Hello,' Turk said. 'Someone abandoned ship in a hurry.

There's an oilskin cap and a thermos flask — and a shell through the engine casing.' He was on all fours. 'And a name-plate. Fried. Krupp A.G. Germaniawerft Kiel-Gaarden.' He rose to his knees. 'Ludd, are you still there? Can you see anything odd about the bows?'

Lobby Ludd peered over the gunwhale of the dinghy. 'There's something, sir — if yer could shift yer weight aft, and bring up the bows a bit — ' He waited until Turk had clambered to the stern of the motor-boat. 'Yessir. There's a bulge — about the size of 'arf a football, with a bit sticking out o' the middle. I'd say it was a torpedo warhead, sir, like you thought.'

Turk grunted. 'Well, don't get too close, Ludd, or you'll find out for certain.' Both boats rose and fell together. 'Now, listen, Ludd — in case I'm not around to explain later. I don't think this is radio-activated. As far as I can see, it's an ordinary motor-boat with a six-cylinder Benz engine driving twin screws, intended to be aimed at a target and then abandoned by its crewmen. It has minimal cockpit controls — manual steering, ignition, throttle, choke, a small magnetic compass, and what seems to be a gyroscopic course stabilizer. Have you got that? There is no access to the bows from the cockpit, so that means that the warhead is fitted and primed from the outside — probably a watertight recess.'

The boat rolled and he drew breath. From the LCF, now almost a hundred yards distant, came Summers's voice over the loud-hailer. 'Is everything all right? You're drifting southeastward. Do you want us to close you?'

Turk signalled a negative and then began to inflate his lifebelt. 'I'm going over the side for a closer look at that warhead, Ludd. It can't be very complicated if it has to be primed on the deck of an E-boat, perhaps in darkness. It ought to be possible to unship the detonator horn.' He carried an assortment of tools in a soap-bag hung from his neck — a small, plastic reticule with a draw-string, commonly used by men to contain their soap and other toiletry articles. 'And this time — as soon as I've shouted what I intend doing — you'll pull well clear.' He glanced at his feet. 'I suppose I might as well take off my slippers, in case I lose 'em.'

Lobby Ludd watched as Turk lowered himself awkwardly into the sea 'Christ it's cold,' he gasped. 'You'd never think it was July.'

There was another hail from the LCF. 'Are you sure you're all right? We're losing sight of you.' Neither Turk nor Ludd responded. Turk clung to the side of the motor-boat, hand-hauling himself towards the bows as the craft rose and plunged in the swell. 'Ludd,' he shouted. 'Can you hear me? I've reached the warhead — a standard twenty-one-inch, I'd say — just the head with the exploder charger, primer and detonator horn, clamped into a cavity.' His voice was a jerky pant. 'The horn's held by a six-sided steel nut, still greased, about two-inch — but probably metric. I'm going to use an adjustable wrench, anti-clockwise.' He turned his face, already bluelipped. 'Off you go, then, Ludd — and row like a mad stoker — '

Lobby Ludd could no longer see the LCF through the mist, but he turned the dinghy on one oar, for the second time. He was chilled to his skin; it must be soddin' cold in the 'ogwash. Yer'd think, he seethed, that someone on the ship would have the bleedin' sense to switch on the twelve-inch lamp. In this visibility a bloke could clew up in Blackpool. And it would serve them bleedin' right; except for a number of cork floats, which were completely unnavigable, the dinghy was the LCF's only boat. He'd like to see 'em all going ashore in their tiddley suits on bleedin' cork floats.

Momentarily, he had lost sight of Turk also, hidden by the overhang of the motor-boat's bows, and he stopped rowing. It was a soddin' lousy trick, leaving anyone like this, even if he was an officer who was paid for it. Turk, he reckoned, was attempting the near-impossible — removing a sensitive detonator with a wrench in one hand, clinging with the other to the side of a lurching hull, cold and wretchedly soaked, and it was even money he'd be blown to pieces. The dinghy was pitching uncomfortably, and he shivered. A bloke deserved better than that, even if he was a bleedin' officer. The heaving motor-boat hull still hid Turk from sight; he could have succumbed to the sea already.

'Sod it,' Ludd spat. Sod this for a skylark.

'Is everything all right?' the distant, muffled loud-hailer enquired. 'We have lost sight of you.'

Lobby Ludd pulled off his shoes. 'HOs', he told the world at large, 'give me the screaming shits.' The dinghy was an unstable platform from which to dive. He lifted himself over the transom and half-jumped, half-fell into the sea.

Soddin' hell. It was colder than charity, and that was bleedin' chilly. The breath was wrenched from his lungs, and he experienced an overwhelming desire to scramble back into the boat, but he was lifted clear, out of reach. The motor-boat was ten yards away, wallowing low in the water, and he struck out, cursing at the stupidity of it. Soddin' hell. Swimming, at any time, was not an activity he held in high regard. He had swum his obligatory test in the training establishment of St George — two freestyle lengths of the pool and one on his back, dressed in a duck suit, then diving for bricks on the pool bottom — but his service in the Arctic, where a man in the water survived for only seconds, had generated an aversion to swimming of any kind. It was time for a bloke to swim when he bleedin' had to. Now he ought to be on the mess-deck with his banger and red lead.

It was too soddin' late now. In for a penny, in for a bleedin' pound. Lieutenant Turk was clinging to the bows of the motor-boat, but only just.

'What the bloody hell are you up to, Ludd? Christ — ' He was white-faced, and with his forearm he was wiping from his eyes the blood that came from a wound hidden by his plastered hair. It had been the eighth roller, Lobby Ludd guessed Inexplicably, every eighth roller was bigger and fiercer than its fellows; everyone knew it, but it always caught a bloke by surprise. 'Ludd I told you to pull clear — '

Lobby Ludd clenched his hands on the ship's rubbing-strake and gulped air. His legs were immediately sucked under the hull, and this weren't a bleedin' skylark any longer. 'Shave off,' he said.

'Ludd — ' Turk choked, then began to vomit.

'I reckoned, sir,' Lobby Ludd panted, 'yer might need a bit of 'elp.' Talking was difficult. It was soddin' cold.

Turk nodded. 'It needs two hands. If you can get closer, Ludd, and hook an elbow around my neck — that's it. Now, I'll manage the wrench if you can adjust it to the horn. Easy, Ludd.' He began to cough. 'Sorry — that's fine — as tight as you can get it. All right — ' Lobby Ludd's fingers were starting to numb, and the boat was climbing three or four feet with each roller and crashing into the following trough with a force that threatened to throw them off again and again, but then Turk emitted a satisfied croak. 'That'll do it, Ludd. We're bloody home and dry, one way or the other.' Lobby Ludd transferred his free hand to the haft of the wrench, reinforcing Turk's. His arm muscles felt like jelly. 'Now,' Turk said. 'Anti-clockwise — when I say. Wait for the next trough. Ready?' He paused. 'Now.'

They both flung their weight upwards against the motion of the hull as it rolled from the wave-crest. The sea dragged them down as the bows reared again, yawed, flung Lobby Ludd aside with a battering-ram blow that left him stunned, winded, and struggling desperately to regain the surface and a lungful of air. Turk had shouted, and he clung to the boat still, his nails torn, but the wrench had gone. Both men blasphemed.

It had been the soddin' eighth roller again, Lobby Ludd supposed. And the wrench was lost. He grappled for another handhold; they snarled at each other.

'Ludd,' Turk gritted, 'we might have loosened it. Give it a try, will you? I'd do it, but I'm bloody well licked. If you can get a hand to it' — he retched again — 'but for Christ's sake be careful. Just see if it turns. If it does, then wait.'

After this, Lobby Ludd vowed, jes' let anyone ask him ter go ter the bleedin' seaside, that's all. He hung by his left hand, a knee each side of the boat's bows, then groped with his right hand for the warhead. It would be easy if the soddin' thing would jes' keep still. The detonator retaining nut filled his hand, but his hand ached with cramp, impotent. The boat climbed, plunged, and Turk's teeth were bared, his eyes clenched, his head still bleeding.

'It's turning, sir,' Lobby Ludd choked. 'It's loose.'

Turk opened his eyes and grinned. 'Bloody good show, Ludd. Now listen. Keep turning it, slowly. When the thread disengages, draw the detonator horn out carefully and straight — as straight as you can. You'll be drawing out the detonator behind the horn, and then a long rod — about eighteen inches — that runs through the exploder charge. Got it? All right. When you've got the whole thing out and clear, drop it like hot shit.'

You ain't bleedin' flannelling, mate, Lobby Ludd mused. The big retaining nut turned easily on its greased thread — more easily than was comfortable — and it seemed endless. He half-inched it in the cup of his aching hand each time the boat momentarily steadied. How long was this soddin' thread? Shave off. There was limits to the time a bloke could swing on one arm like a soddin' baboon. And if the detonator went off now, he'd lose his pills fer certain. Turk, white-faced and plainly exhausted, watched him in silence.

Then, at last, he sensed the nut's loosening coherence that told him that the nut's interlocking threads were about to separate. It was about bleedin' time. He drew a breath, waited until the boat settled in a long trough, and gave a final, determined twist of his wrist. The detonator horn came clearly away from the warhead, behind it the long, metal rod that Turk had described, leaving an open, cylindrical aperture. Lobby Ludd brandished his prize as the boat heeled crazily. 'Give the bloke a coconut!' he panted exultantly, and flung it with the last of his strength.

Turk was laughing. 'Christ,' he jerked, 'I'm glad I was right about that detonator, Ludd. All I know about torpedo warheads is what I remember from a diagram in Modern Boy, about ten years ago.'

They regained the dinghy and secured the motor-boat with the painter, then waited, shivering. The mist seemed to have thickened. Turk, from the German compass, knew the bearing of the French coast, the nearest point of which lay twenty miles away, almost due south, but they could not guess where the LCF was. There was little to be gained by rowing, even if either was capable. Turk's appearance was ghastly; his head wound had stopped bleeding and he said it no longer hurt, but his face was crimson-smeared, his lips slate-coloured. It wouldn't do, Lobby Ludd supposed, to tell an officer he looked like bleedin' Frankenstein. He kept quiet. Christ, it was cold. And he was soddin' hungry.

'You'd think, Ludd,' calculated Turk, 'that there'd be so many bloody ships in this area of the Channel they'd be bouncing off each other.' And not forgetting LCF49, Lobby Ludd simmered, where they were all stuffing themselves with bangers and red lead.

'In case you ain't noticed, sir,' he ventured, 'we've lost an oar.'

'I've just remembered.' Turk groped under his thwart. 'I left my cigarettes and matches in my starboard slipper.' He offered the damp package to Lobby Ludd. 'I shouldn't be surprised if you get a medal, Ludd. I'm going to recommend a DSM for your determination.'

It had not occurred to Lobby Ludd; he was surprised but not elated. 'That'd be fine, sir, thanks,' he nodded, then returned his attention to the mist-floating sea to northward. A medal. It was bleedin' funny, he thought, how only officers were capable of heroism or gallantry; they were rewarded with orders or crosses. Ratings had to be satisfied with medals because they could only display determination and devotion to duty.

Turk was mildly surprised at Ludd's indifference. It had probably been a mistake to mention it. Anyway, a recommendation from a Lieutenant RNR was unlikely to carry much weight and would probably be lost among the hundreds of similar reports pouring into SHAEF. It was bloody funny, he thought, how much more a decoration meant to an officer than to a rating — probably because, in later years, nobody would guess that Fred in the stores had once served a gun single-handed, or flung himself on an unexploded shell to save his ship, and his medals would be tarnishing in a drawer among old birthday cards and holiday snapshots. The retired officer would order minatures from Gieves or Alkit and sport them on his dress jacket at the executives' annual dinner because the chairman had an OBE for services to industry and liked to show it off for the benefit of the staff magazine.

'There's engine noises, sir.' They both listened. 'An ML or an MTB.' It was difficult to tell from which direction the noise was coming, but they agreed on north-west. 'Try a hail, Ludd,' Turk said. 'They might hear.'

'Ahoy, there!' Lobby Ludd shouted through cupped hands. 'Ship ahoy!' It sounded like the words of a comic song.

The boat that emerged slowly from the swirl of mist to northward was neither an ML nor an MTB. It was bigger than either — a mastless, grey-green vessel with a low, open bridge, guns forward and aft, and the fluted bow-flanks that both recognized immediately. There was a stubby jack amidships, but its ensign hung limply, unidentifiable. 'Christ,' Turk choked. 'It's an E-boat.'

They both stared, involuntarily crouching, as if that might make their dinghy appear smaller. The rumble of diesel engines came to them clearly, and they could see men on the bridge and on deck, indistinct in the mist but very real. Then, as suddenly as it had appeared, the stranger glided into a curtain of grey vapour and in seconds had gone from sight.

'Shave off.' Lobby Ludd breathed, hardly believing it. The throb of engines faded. 'One of His Majesty's dinghies was nearly reported missing. Yer ain't thinking of giving chase, are yer, sir?'

Turk was still staring in the direction of the vanished E-boat. 'What's it doing? These waters must be swarming with Trout Line craft — not to mention the odd destroyer or two. That German commander should have been back in Le Havre or Brest hours ago. He's either a very brave man, Ludd, or a bloody stupid one.'

Lobby Ludd was flattered that Turk should confide in him, but for the moment the question seemed wholly academic. He clenched his teeth to stop their chattering. 'P'raps he's lost, sir,' he sniffed. Like soddin' LCF49. The only important thing, he thought, was that the E-boat didn't bleedin' come back. 'Or p'raps he was looking fer his motor-boat, and the bloke that ain't driving it.'

'In that case he spent too long looking,' Turk nodded. 'He's been caught in the open at dawn and he's cut off from his base. I would have thought his best bet was to get further to seaward, clear of this mist, and make a dash for Le Havre. He must have all of forty knots.' He paused. 'Unless he's damaged.'

Lobby Ludd was even less concerned than before. He was on his feet, bawling, as the ugly bows of LCF49 nosed into view only sixty yards away.

'Ahoy, LCF!'

The dinghy rocked, and the ship's loud-hailer flared. 'We have you in sight. Am closing you, port side to.' They could see men running forward on the well-deck — Walt with a heaving line, Lieutenant Taplow and several Marines. The dinghy rolled again as the ship's bow wave lifted it, but the line came snaking down, and Turk was already shouting orders.

'Sound off action stations, Taplow. There's an E-boat — probably a mile to eastward by now. Get Henry. I want to make an enemy report.' He was clambering aboard. 'Get these two boats hoisted inboard; the motor-boat's safe. Where's the wardroom steward? I want a dry change of clothes brought to the bridge, at the rush — and some hot breakfast. Ludd, off you go, man. Get cleaned and be back on deck as quick as you can. Ah, Bunter, load all guns and stand by to engage surface target ... '

*

'We've had a reply to your first signal to C-in-C Portsmouth, sir,' Summers reported. 'We should "not repeat not interfere with torpedo craft mechanism", but merely keep it under surveillance. Two experts from the Torpedo School are being despatched in the escort destroyer Toreador, which will rendezvous with us at about noon.'

'We're keeping it under surveillance, on the after-deck,' Turk nodded. He gulped at scalding coffee generously laced with rum. 'Ah, Ludd. Pour yourself some of this. It'll put a curl in your tonsils. Number One, steer oh-seven-oh until we clear this mist. It's my guess the E-boat's doing the same — trying to tip-toe back to Le Havre in bad visibility. He must have engine trouble, or he would have run for it at full throttle, and nothing of ours could have caught him. If that's so, and if this mist is only local — and if we can be waiting for him when he puts out his nasty little nose — '

'I read a story like this once,' Perk told Walt, 'in the Wizard. There was this bloke Tusker Gordon, see, and another bloke that was a Gurkha. He 'ad a bleedin' cricket bat. They was fightin' the invaders from Mars, with skins like fish an' silver blood. They paralysed the soddin' navy fer a start.'

'Then they put 'em in tins,' Walt agreed, 'and called 'em 'errins-in. They still paralyse the soddin' navy.'

Turk was gingerly patting his head with a towel. 'I've got a thumping bloody headache, that's all. Peach can have a go at it later. Wheel-house — full ahead both. Bring her around to oh-five-five, cox'sn.' He cupped several aspirin tablets into his mouth. 'It'd help if we knew where we were. I'd say we're twenty — twenty-five miles north-west of Deauville, which means we're in tiger country. It's an enemy-held coastline, with eleven-inch gun batteries that could chew us to arse-paper in a few seconds — if they sight us.' He winced, but waved away Peach who was hovering with his first-aid haversack. 'And the E-boat commander will know that better than us. He could run for the yacht basin at Deauville, but he won't. He'll make for Le Havre, where he came from.' He took another mouthful of coffee. 'But not if we can bloody stop him, Number One. I want him nailed and stuffed. Ludd — if you drink any more of that coffee, you'll be pissy-kacky … '

'O' course,' ERA Gilbert complained to Stoker Bowles, 'nobody cares about my bleedin' wrench that's lorst. Whose soddin' slop chit is that going on? What do I say when I get my next tool muster? — that the skipper lorst it when he was swimmin'?'

On the forward mess-deck SBA Peach opened the medicine chest and unfolded his rubber sheets and blankets.

The mist cleared suddenly, as if it had been torn aside. It still lay astern, curtaining the Normandy coast, but ahead the sea was clear and blue, glinting in the sunshine, silver stippled. To starboard was the wide Seine estuary with a coastline just visible — the merest thread of grey on a distant horizon. There were gulls overhead, and the breeze was warm.

LCF49, however, was no longer alone. Off her port bow, two miles to seaward, was the slowly crawling shape of the E-boat.

Eight

Nothing happened immediately. The two vessels were on similar courses, approximately parallel to the coast, with the E-boat obliquely ahead of the LCF. One fact, however, was instantly apparent to the British as it must have been equally to the enemy commander; given parity of speed and manoeuvre the LCF stood between the E-boat and her Le Havre base.

Under normal circumstances the advantage would have meant little. In an emergency, and for brief periods, LCF49 could achieve twelve knots; she was tactically cumbersome. The E-boat was capable of at least forty knots and could turn almost in her own length. She could open her throttles and show a clean pair of heels to almost any British craft afloat.

The possibility of being cornered by a lumbering, square-bowed hybrid like the LCF49 was laughable.

On this occasion, however, there was no distant roar of triple diesels, no creaming wake. The E-boat was moving and a belch of exhaust smoke momentarily obscured her stern, but her speed did not increase.

'She's on one engine!' Turk shouted, ran for the chart table, then stabbed a finger eastward. 'That's Cap d'Antifer. If he wants to get into Le Havre he'll have to make a dog-leg turn — and if he does, we've got him, Number One.'

Summers was less confident. He had his glasses on the E-boat. 'She's got an after 37-mm, sir, which is probably better than our pom-poms — apart from twin 20-mm forward. I'd say she can slightly outrange our guns, even if we have more of them. Apart from that' — he glanced up — 'she's got two twenty-one-inch torpedoes. That could be nasty.' The E-boat, he was reminding Turk, carried a sting. She could inflict punishing damage before the LCF's heavier broadside overwhelmed her, and, if she could bring her torpedo tubes to bear, the result could be disastrous.

'That commander is probably weighing the same odds,' Turk nodded. 'Unless he's bluffing — which I doubt — he hasn't the shaft-power for any rapid manoeuvring. If he turns to use his tubes, his after gun won't bear, but he'll not risk his torpedoes at this range, Number One.' He calculated. 'Now — you see. If we threaten to close, he'll turn his stern. He doesn't want a rough-house. If he can't get into Le Havre he'll try for somewhere farther up-coast — perhaps Dieppe. We've got to cat-and-mouse him into mid-Channel, out of range of those eleven-inch shore batteries. Bunter — stand by.' He took another cigarette from a crumpled packet. 'Port ten. Emergency full ahead.'

The sights of all guns bearing had been locked on to the distant target for several minutes. Now the muzzles turned as the LCF49 heeled and a tumble of black smoke broke from her funnel. 'She's firing, sir,' Summers said, binoculars raised. There was another puffball of smoke two miles to the north east and then, distinctly audible, the slow chuk-chuk-chuk of the E-boat's 37-mm gun.

'He's short,' Turk grunted, 'but not that much. 'No, we're not going to let him know what our guns can do.' He turned to the wheel-house voice-pipe. 'Starboard ten, cox'sn. Steer oh-four-oh. What's your reckoning, Bunter?'

Lieutenant Bunter, on the Lewis gun platform abaft the bridge, had been sighting the enemy through a small hand range-finder that gave a crude indication of distance in cables. He shook his head. 'He's got the edge on us, sir. As you say, it's not much, but all the time he keeps his distance he can just outrange us. It all depends on how fast we can close the range when he's going away — '

*

It was a beautiful July morning, with the sky clear and blue, the sun warm, and a fresh breeze off the green, white-tipped rollers that tingled in the nostrils. It was a morning that, in more peaceful times, would have seen the Channel between Deauville and Fécamp dancing with the bellying spinnakers of yachts, crawling with coastal freighters, harbour craft and ferries. Today the crews of only two vessels — two of the less noteworthy of their respective navies — regarded each other malevolently across two miles of water. Turk was surprised that the area should be so deserted. He had expected to sight either British minesweepers with escorting destroyers or, less welcome, patrolling enemy forces from the Seine estuary, but perhaps this was one of those no-man's stretches of sea that both sides chose to ignore for reasons not apparent to a Lieutenant RNR.

For the moment there was stalemate. Each time the LCF narrowed the range, the E-boat opened fire with her after 37-mm cannon; the Germans' gun-laying was excellent, and on each occasion Turk turned away.

'The bastard's aiming at me,' Walt complained. 'I'spose they know who to go for, after that chimney.'

Bunter swore impatiently, and Turk chuckled. 'I know what you're thinking, Bunter. Well, you can forget it. I know we've got twelve guns to his three, but we can bring only six to bear, and he has his torpedoes. He's opened his tube doors, but he can't present his bows because that nullifies his thirty-seven millimetre.' He had his binoculars to his eyes. 'We're preventing him turning towards shore, but we can't close him without first getting a kick in the teeth. A blaze of glory is fine, Bunter, but dead heroes have wives and kids who never seem to understand. So,' he nodded, 'we'll see what a little patience can do. We've got all day.'

Three times in the next hour Turk increased speed and turned the LCF towards the E-boat off his port bow, and three times the enemy veered away with a warning burst of gunfire. Telegraphist Henry brought a decoded signal to the bridge. 'It was broadcast by Portsmouth W/T, sir,' he reported '"Report your position."'

'It means that Toreador can't find us where she thinks we ought to be,' Turk mused. He sucked his teeth. 'Well, a destroyer could settle this business easier than kiss your arse, Number One, but it could be just what the enemy is expecting. What do you think?'

Summers thought. 'You mean we're being used as bait?'

'We're only guessing that E-boat has engine trouble — but she has a radio, hasn't she? It's bloody odd, after all this, that nothing's come pounding out of Le Havre or Dieppe at a rate of knots. I doubt whether the RAF has destroyed all the radar sites on this stretch of coast, and those German eleven-inch coastal batteries are said to be accurate to within ten yards of a target at twenty miles. Add that together, Number One, and the answer could be that someone's waiting for a destroyer — or hopefully half a flotilla — to come galloping up singing "Rosemary". Then — bingo!'

'I'd never have thought of that,' Summers conceded. It seemed too involved to be likely.

'I didn't think of it myself until it occurred to me that this E-boat commander wasn't exactly rupturing himself in trying to make harbour. The Germans are bloody good at this sort of thing, Number One. Ask Ludd about the Susquehanna. She was a transport full of German POWs that was torpedoed in error. Then, with three thousand of their own countrymen in the sea, the U-boats waited for British and American warships to begin picking up survivors. One U-boat even broadcast a truce.' Obliquely consulted, Lobby Ludd nodded and narrowed his eyes grimly. It hadn't occurred to him, either, until now.

'If we're going ter get thumped wi' a bleedin' eleven-inch shell,' Perk told Walt, 'I 'ope it's after tot-time. Bowlesey owes me 'arf.'

'And I've got my dhobeying 'ung in the paint locker,' Walt agreed.

'Bunter,' Turk decided, 'I want you to tell your gun crews that next time we turn to port we're going to keep going, hell for leather. If we're lucky, the enemy will turn away, fire his burst then expect us to resume course — the mixture as before. It could take several seconds before he realizes we're still coming, and opens fire again. Then you can let him have everything you've got, whether you reach or not. Understand? He's got to decide whether to continue firing his thirty-seven millimetre or turn to present his tubes. If his engines are sick, he'll not turn in a hurry, and we'll have him nailed; if he's bluffing, then God help us. All the same, that gun can be very spiteful. Loading numbers are not to expose themselves; I don't want any bravado just because they think they've done it all before. And that includes Taplow — and you, Number One. There are seventy-five men on this ship, and I want to take seventy-five men home.'

'C-in-C Portsmouth's getting stroppy, sir,' Telegraphist Henry advised. 'Operational Priority — "Report your position immediately." I had to transmit, and I shouldn't be surprised if we've been pinned down by D/F. It won't take Toreador long to locate us, sir.'

Turk grunted. 'All right, Sparks. Code up a signal for C-in-C, repeated Commander Allied Naval Expeditionary Force and Toreador. "Am pursuing surface contact probably E-boat position approximately twenty miles north-west of Étretat." That ought to tell Toreador that we're within range of the enemy's coastal heavies — '

'Toreador's calling on VHF, sir,' Lobby Ludd interrupted. '"Am closing you on D/F bearing but slowed by heavy mist. Have two small vessels on radar screen ahead six miles. Presume you are one. Who is the other?"'

'Six miles? Bugger it,' Turk said. 'He's going to explode into view at any moment — and I'll lay a pound to a stoker's sock that the German's gunnery radar's got him nicely measured for a new suit. These destroyer types think the sun shines out of their bloody stern brackets. Ludd, tell Toreador: "Am about to engage E-boat within range of coastal batteries —"' He stopped, then, 'No, don't tell him anything.' He whirled. 'Bunter, are you ready? It's got to be first time, you understand?'

As the smoke from her funnel thickened, LCF49 swung to port, her deck tilting. Instantly, as before, the distant E-boat turned away and gun smoke hazed her stern as she fired — a burst of five shots, a pause, then another five — with the projectiles striking the sea like flung gravel fifty yards ahead of the assault craft.

'Steady cox'sn,' Turk shouted. 'Hold her as she is. I want the target on the bow, so all guns can bear.' The LCF's prow smashed squarely through a roller and spray drenched the forward gun positions. 'Not yet, Bunter,' Turk warned.

The E-boat's gun was silent for a further moment and then realization dawned on the enemy. Through his glass Lobby Ludd could see the German commander on his small bridge, staring aft and mouthing orders through cupped hands. Forward, two crewmen had manned the twin 20-mm, while a third and fourth wrestled with a light machine-gun at the bridge screen. Again, the enemy's stern was shrouded in smoke as the after gun resumed firing, and this time the fall of shot was menacingly closer. The E-boat, wallowing, was not the most stable of gun platforms, but the LCF was closing the range and growing larger in the German's sights with every second. On the vibrating fore-deck the marines were hunched behind their guns, tensed, and Bunter glanced at Turk.

A vicious flurry of 37-mm shells lashed off the sea like pebbles and punched through the 3/8 inch steel of the LCF's side as if it was paper.

'If that shamfered the soddin' paint locker,' Walt threatened, 'I'll bleedin' shave off, mate.'

Perk nodded grimly. 'Or the soddin' rum store.'

Lobby Ludd heard the armoured deadlights of the wheel-house below crash shut, and then he ducked as the twelve-inch lamp swung like a top on its mounting, shattered and flung glass across the bridge. The canvas canopy over the flag locker was shredded, and wooden splinters flew from a wrecked chart table. 'Christ,' Turk shouted. 'All right, Bunter — open fire!'

The crews and loading numbers, protected only by their flimsy gun-shields, had been waiting desperately for the order, and the port battery fired on the ship's downward roll with the broadside of six guns erupting into a continuous, pounding roar. The inevitable pall of stinging smoke was flung back over the gun positions, but it flattened and then thinned as the ship rose again. Beyond the smoke the snaking ribbons of tracer were reaching out like incandescent tendrils, converging, towards the E-boat, first falling a hundred yards short and tearing the sea to angry froth, but moving closer as the gunners found their range. The acrid reek of cordite was choking, the noise deafening. On the fore-deck Taplow flung himself to hands and knees as an enemy shot struck the open hatch-cover of the magazine and ricocheted into oblivion. Men prised open ammunition boxes, crouched low, and the forward pom-pom had ceased fire with a round jammed in the breech. Its crewmen were wrenching off the magazine plate and shouting for the ordnance artificer. Turk peered ahead with eyes narrowed and an unlit stub of a cigarette between his lips. 'He's a stubborn bastard,' he yelled, and then he blasphemed. 'He's going away!'

There was a white tumble at the E-boat's stern, her bows were lifting, and the distance separating her from the LCF was already widening. 'Well, fer pissing down the sink,' Walt retorted disgustedly. 'And I ain't 'ad a bleedin' shot yet. If I'd 'ad a shot, mate, we'd be draggin' out the soddin' survivors by now.'

'Cease fire!' Turk ordered. He smashed a fist into a palm. 'Either he's repaired his engines, right on cue, or there was nothing wrong with them in the first place.' He was explosively angry. 'Ludd, call Toreador on VHF. Tell her — '

'The VHF set's bust, sir,' Lobby Ludd reported, amazed. The VHF radio, less than an arm's length from him, had been smashed to twisted scrap by a direct hit, but he had not known. It just went to show.

Turk swore again. 'That's just bloody fine,' he said. The E-boat was circling to eastward, well out of range, at twice the LCF's speed. 'Number One, let me have a damage report — at the rush. Bunter, keep the guncrews on their toes. We may not be finished yet.' His binoculars were on the retreating enemy, and then he turned them astern. 'Oh, shit —'

A destroyer — and it could only be Toreador — had emerged from the mist haze astern and was overhauling the LCF with incredible rapidity, her bow wave creaming high as she thrust easily through the sea, her single funnel vomiting. There was a distant whoop-whoop of a siren, and Lobby Ludd reached for his Aldis lamp just as the destroyer's foreward turret crashed twice. 'Signal, sir,' he shouted. '"You really ought to leave this sort of thing to the big boys."' Turk tore the dead cigarette from his mouth and snarled. 'Very funny, but if that E-boat was just trailing his coat for the benefit of his shore batteries, that destroyer cowboy is going to get a bloody shock, any second now.'

Toreador was already abeam, then surging ahead with effortless arrogance, her forward twin four-inch guns firing steadily, each at a rate of fifteen rounds per minute. Northward, the E-boat was weaving among a spatter of shell-splashes, and the LCF's crew watched with mixed feelings — of anticipation of the enemy's destruction and annoyance that they had been robbed of the pleasure of achieving it.

Summers had climbed to the bridge. 'As far as I can count, sir, we've sustained fourteen hits on the hull — all thirty-seven millimetre. Four have penetrated to the Marines' locker flat forward and are taking water, but they're being plugged. The paint locker's a shambles' —

'Screw a pig,' Walt moaned.

— 'and the wireman's workshop. Otherwise, apart from the wheelhouse, bridge and funnel, it's all superficial. There's no casualties except SBA Peach.'

'SBA Peach?'

Summers nodded. 'When he heard the four shells come through the locker flat he thought we'd been torpedoed, and was sick in the sterilizer — but he'll live.' He grinned.

Then he stopped grinning. There was a sudden, awful noise that made the senses cringe — a swelling, rasping whine like the noise of an express train approaching from a distance at high speed, directly at the listener — and every man on the fore-deck and bridge listened. Without exception they froze, as if immobility offered some degree of immunity against the horror that was almost upon them, that they all recognized immediately but prayed to be mistaken about. There was nowhere to run, nowhere to hide.

Toreador, at speed, was turning to port, heeling forty-five degrees. The whine had become a roar, and then stopped. Beyond and ahead of the destroyer a huge white column of spray exploded from the sea, climbed skyward. A second mushroomed just astern.

'She's straddled!' Turk grunted hoarsely. 'That's damn good shooting for a first salvo.' He hammered the palm of his hand against the engine-room bell-push to exhort every possible revolution from the LCF's already labouring diesels. 'Hard to port!'

A single flag streamed from Toreador's yardarm, and Lobby Ludd grappled with an answering pennant. 'From Toreador, sir,' he yelled. '"Take immediate avoiding action!"'

'You can bet your bloody life we will,' Turk vowed. 'Midships, cox'sn, and steady.' He calculated, talking quickly. 'A two-gun battery, eleven-or sixteen-inch naval guns. I'd guess they're firing at extreme range — say one salvo a minute, which means we can expect five or six more salvoes before we're clear.' He lifted his binoculars just as another whine, increasing, warned of the hurtling approach of almost a ton of steel and high explosive. Toreador was to northward, twisting like an eel, as the E-boat had been only minutes before. Her signal lamp was flashing. '"Don't phone us, we'll phone you,"' Lobby Ludd read. The sea erupted twice, close enough to the destroyer — as Perk reported — to scorch the paint off her arse. The shore battery, firing by radar, was seeking Toreador first; there would be time for the smaller fry, the LCF, later.

'Why ain't the RAF bombed the sods?' Perk asked; but the RAF was seeking enemy VI missile sites and had few resources to spare for massively protected shore batteries that, so far, had caused little annoyance to anyone except the navy; and if the navy did not like the batteries, then its ships should not go near them.

'Fifty-five seconds between salvoes,' Summers said.

Turk nodded. 'And say thirty seconds' flight time, at least. Ludd, as soon as the next salvo falls, count off thirty seconds and shout. We'll alter course. Bunter, get your crews behind cover. The enemy's firing HE, and there could be splinters from near misses.'

There was a scream of shells, and they stared ahead as the missiles fell. 'Toreador's out of range,' Summers suggested. 'We're next.' Lobby Ludd watched the jerking second hand of the deck clock. Five, ten, fifteen ...

'Thirty seconds, sir,' he shouted.

Turk waited for what seemed an uncomfortably prolonged length of time. If the enemy was about to engage LCF49 he would need to re-range. 'Starboard twenty.' Ashore, an electronics brain would be computing the LCF's distance, course and speed allowing for wind, barometer pressure, corrected muzzle velocity and drift, to ensure that the shells fell on the predicted position of the target, thirty or forty seconds after the guns had been fired. Once the shells were in flight, however, they were committed, and nothing could be done if the target suddenly changed its course or speed. Unfortunately the LCF's meagre twelve knots and her clumsy handling characteristics made her a poor instrument for finely timed evasive tactics.

*

Below, seated at the controls between the two pounding engines, Stoker Bowles stared at the revolutions gauge, willing the trembling needle to climb deeper into the red segment of the dial that indicated emergency speed. His throttle levers were pushed hard forward against their stops, and he held both hands against them. ERA Gilbert stood behind him with feet braced on the juddering deck-plates. The noise was deafening and the reek of hot oil stung in the throat. They could only guess what was happening above deck, and they guessed that the situation was critical, perhaps perilous. Emergency speed was a luxury to be used sparingly, to be carefully recorded in the engine-room log. The strain on the hammering pistons, crankshafts, clutches and propeller shafts was vicious, and there was good reason for the ERA'S narrowed eyes and the sweat in the creases of his face. The big Paxman diesels were being driven to the limit of their safe capacity.

Above Bowles's head the two telegraph repeaters suddenly clang-clanged and their pointers whirled angrily. The bridge was demanding another fifty revolutions on each screw, and Bowles turned an imploring face, mouthed an obscenity — his voice would have been inaudible — and nodded at his hard-over throttle levers. ERA Gilbert hesitated, sucked in his breath, then drew a screwdriver from an overall pocket and began deliberately to remove the safety stop that bridged the levers under Bowles's hands. Stoker Bowles stared, unbelieving. He drew a finger across his throat, placed his hands together in supplication, and lifted his eyes to the heavens beyond the vibrating deck-head.

*

'For what we are about to receive ... ' Turk muttered, as they heard the approach of the next salvo and tensed every muscle. In the next few seconds remaining any attempt to anticipate anything was futile; cohesive thought was almost impossible. A shell burst in the sea to port, then a second, a mere fifty yards distant. Two distinct reverberations shuddered the ship as if it was made of pasteboard, and invisible splinters hummed through the air, rattled against the superstructure and gouged at the puny coamings encircling each gun position behind which the gunners crouched. Several feet of a riveted seam in the funnel were torn open to spill black engine smoke over the after-deck. 'Yer bloody missed!' Walt jeered, shaking his fist, but more relieved than his belligerence suggested. Lobby Ludd wrenched his attention back to the deck clock. Five, ten, fifteen ...

'It worked once,' Turk said, 'but it might not a second time, Number One.' The enemy battery commander could delay his firing until the target's change of course became apparent, and he could spread the line of his salvo to improve the probability of one shell hitting; it would require only one to reduce the LCF to a twisted shambles.

Summers shouted, 'Sir! Toreador's turned! She's coming back into range!'

Turk whirled. 'Good God, so she is.' They could see only the destroyer's slimmest profile, but there was no mistaking the narrow V of her bows with the white ferment of spume lifting away on each flank, which meant that she steered directly for the LCF. For a confused moment Turk grappled for the reason; there could be only one. Toreador was returning to draw the shore battery's fire on herself.

'I'll take back all I said,' Turk marvelled. 'These destroyer types don't all think the sun shines out of their stern brackets. Only some of 'em. Ludd, she's flashing.'

Lobby Ludd would have liked to explain that to read the seconds off the deck clock and simultaneously read a morse signal from the flag-deck of a distant destroyer was an undertaking beyond his capabilities, but soddin' officers never thought before they shouted.

'Will you walk a little faster said a whiting to a snail,' the light blinked. 'There's a porpoise close behind us and he's treading on my — '

Lobby Ludd cursed, but Toreador was heeling as she passed astern, turning into a wide circle. There were few sights more dramatic than a destroyer at high speed, and a cheer came from the fore-deck. It was clear that the manoeuvre had momentarily confused the shore battery; the interval of time since the last salvo had lengthened to more than two minutes, but it could not last.

'Just another mile,' Summers implored. 'One mile, and we're clear.'

Toreador was buying time, but the cost to herself could be terrible. The LCF's mangled funnel gushed smoke from a dozen ragged holes, and the shudder of her decks was so vehement that Turk suspected the ERA was pushing the engines beyond their designed potential. He hoped, by Christ, that Gilbert knew what he was doing, because a breakdown now would be disastrous.

They could hear the whine of shells for the fifth time. If they survived this salvo, Lobby Ludd promised God, he would never again evade Sunday Divisions and divine service by pretending to be Scottish Free Church and Other Denominations, but the law of averages said that, of ten shells fired, one must surely find its mark.

One did.

'Toreador's hit, sir!' he bellowed, guiltily relieved that it was someone else. The destroyer, having achieved an almost complete half-circle to shoreward of the LCF, had obviously sustained damage. She had slowed noticeably. There was an immense, dense eruption of steam amidships, and the uninterrupted screech of escaping vapour was easily audible across the thousand yards that separated her from the labouring assault craft.

'That's put a few quid on her slop chit,' Perk observed.

'Ludd — ask her if she needs assistance — ' Turk stopped. 'No, don't. We'll wait.' The question could be interpreted as gloating. 'Number One. Muster a fire party and break out hoses, then stand by aft to take a line from Toreador — just in case we have to tow her.' The situation was getting complicated.

Within moments, however, Toreador's signal lamp was blinking. 'Shell burst in number one boiler room and badly damaged main feed tank. Reduced to half speed. Casualties not yet assessed but I can cope. Keep going.'

'Watch her, Ludd,' Turk warned. 'We might still have to go about.'

Lieutenant Bunter was gauging distance. 'It's just Toreador now, sir. She's only making about ten knots, and she might just be within range of another salvo. I think we're out of the wood.'

'Well, that's clewed up, then,' Perk told Walt. 'It must be nearly tot time, mate. If I don't get down there early, Bowlesey'll ferget about my 'arf. It's funny 'ow he always bleedin' fergets.'

'I jes' can't face going down the paint locker,' Walt sniffed. 'Mind, I ain't worried about all my dhobeying that's soddin' ruined. It's all that lovely bleedin' paint that's wasted.'

There was one last salvo, and they waited for the shells to fall, saw the splashes climb astern and clear of the lame destroyer and knew the enemy had shot his bolt. They were safe. Toreador had a list to starboard, but she was making ground, and every yard she clawed took her farther from the enemy coast.

'Estimate I can steam at eight to ten knots for three hours' she flashed. 'Intend making for Portsmouth. Will signal for assistance and report I have taken you under command. Take station astern, course three-two-eight.'

Turk ordered speed reduced. The shudder of the engines eased and the tumble of black smoke from the funnel thinned to an oily haze. The wheel-house deadlights were being opened and ERA Gilbert climbed from the engine-room hatch, wiping his face with a filthy rag. The destroyer was slowly overhauling.

'Ludd, tell the First Lieutenant to secure aft and stand down one watch. Pipe "Up Spirits". Ludd!' Turk frowned. 'What the hell, man? You're standing in blood.'

Lobby Ludd, surprised, stared at his feet. His right shoe oozed blood through its laces and, within, the sock felt warmly sodden. The lower inches of his trouser leg were bloodily wet, and there was spattered blood and crimson footprints on the deck.

'Shave off,' he breathed. 'I didn't feel nothin'.' He grinned. 'I'spect I've only lorst a foot.' And then he thought about it.

'Walters, get the SBA, at the rush,' Turk instructed, 'if he's not being sick. Ludd, sit down, man, before you fall down. Bunter, get some brandy — '

It was a pity about the brandy, Lobby Ludd decided as his senses blurred. There might just be time to say something heroic before he died, if he could think of something, but he couldn't.

*

The big rescue tug met them in mid-Channel to take Toreador in tow, and the trio's progress was slow but uneventful between Bembridge Point and the Nab lightship, past Clarence Pier to starboard and into the five-fathom channel. The weather was fine, and a throng of dockyard workers, drawn to the jetty by the gathered ambulances, watched the causalties being disembarked from the two shell-damaged vessels. Lobby Ludd allowed himself to be transported by stretcher, and waved stoically as Perk promised that, if his leg was amputated, they'd have a collection for a parrot. Multiple lacerations, Peach had told him, mostly from glass splinters, several of which the SBA had extracted, but it was a job for Haslar, not the Marines' mess-deck. A few stitches, a week of immobility, and he would be on his feet with little to show except a few scars and a pair of torn trousers. Lobby Ludd felt pleasantly incapacitated.

'We'll be expecting you back, Ludd,' Turk said. 'If our repairs are completed before you're discharged from RNH, we'll probably get a relief signalman, but I'll let the drafting office know that I want you returned aboard. And you might get a few days' leave. If you do, convey my best wishes to Mrs Ludd.'

'By the time we're out of dock, mate,' Walt calculated, 'the Germans might 'ave surrendered, and we could all get our bleedin' tickets by Christmas.'

'Yer mean we could all be on our way ter the soddin' Far East,' Perk mused, 'ter invade 'Ong Kong. I've always fancied a bit o' Chinese. They 'ave their skirts slit up the sides.'

ERA Gilbert nodded. 'And that ain't all, mate. I can tell yer something else … '

Nine

'You're a long way from the station,' Mrs Ludd accused, straightening her hat with the puce rose-buds, 'and the fare's gone up.' She glanced around the ward and glared at an orderly. 'It's nothing like Queen Charlotte's. When I was in Queen Charlotte's with you' — her voice was loud — 'we had real nurses and a matron.'

Lobby Ludd explained that there were such things as male nurses, and most of them were decent blokes, but Mrs Ludd insisted that it wasn't the same. They didn't look like nurses. The gate porter had told her — firmly, to begin with — that visiting hours were from two till four and nobody was permitted to visit at eleven in the morning, but, threatened by a green umbrella, he decided that regulations could be waived in an emergency, and this was an emergency.

'I don't suppose they give you much to eat,' Mrs Ludd challenged, glaring at the orderly again, and proceeded to fill the shelves of the bedside locker with comestibles that included a slab of cold bread-pudding, a tin of pink salmon and two railway pork pies, then presented a bandage-swathed stoker in the next bed, to his surprise, with a massive wedge of sponge cake. 'I put an egg in that,' she said. 'It will do you good.' He thanked her and said he would eat it later.

When the Wardmaster appeared the orderly froze. The Wardmaster was a formidable person whose administration of a naval hospital was based on a relentlessly maintained timetable, antiseptic floor polish, silence, and no smoking in the wards. He disapproved of visitors at any time, but never before had a visitor interrupted his 11 a.m. rounds and, incredibly, distributed bread-pudding, Woodbines and nutty crunch toffee among the ward's patients. Worse, Mrs Ludd had decided that beds should never be made like this, and was demonstrating to the weakly protesting orderly exactly how they should be.

The Wardmaster narrowed his eyes. 'Madam — '

'Ah,' Mrs Ludd said, and pointed her umbrella. 'Are you in charge? I've been waiting for you. I'm Charlie's mother. Now, these beds — '

'Madam,' the Wardmaster repeated coldly, 'these beds are made in accordance — '

'Don't madam me, young man,' Mrs Ludd ordered, 'and don't tell me about making beds. I was making beds before you were born. And these floors — ' She indicated the immaculately polished maple underfoot. 'It's bare wood. What you need is some nice lino. Even workhouses have lino, and these' — her umbrella swung — 'are our fighting boys. They're entitled to lino.'

He snorted impatiently. 'Lino is not conducive to hygiene. It harbours bacteria.' This, he could see, was one of those women who chained themselves to railings. 'And some of these men are on diets. I cannot allow the unauthorized distribution of' — he glanced at the bread-pudding and raised his eyebrows 'food.'

'Food,' Mrs Ludd nodded. 'I was coming to food, young man.' Her umbrella stabbed to within inches of his nose. 'I know what they get — potato soup, prunes, and gruel — '

'Gruel!' He gaped. 'Madam, lean inform you — '

'I can inform you,' she snapped. 'I've brought up two boys of my own.' She drew herself up to her full sixty-one inches. 'Mark my words, young man. I shall be coming back — and when I do, I shall expect to see some changes. If I don't' — she flourished her umbrella like a cutlass — 'I shall write to Lord Louis Mountbatten.'

*

She hoped he would understand, said the pink letter, and that he could forgive. It wasn't that, after the war, he would still be in the navy; he mustn't think that — even though her mother said that a son-in-law in the navy in wartime was one thing, but in peacetime was something different. She, Freda Harris, didn't think that, not exactly, but there was the future to think about, and Owen Melville did have an assured future with the Borough Engineer's Department, and already had his name on the council's housing list. Being in the town hall, he did enjoy certain advantages.

She hoped that he, Charlie, would not take it too hard; she felt terrible about it, but time healed all wounds. It was fortunate that she did not have to return his ring because he had never given her one. Owen had given her a solitaire. He mustn't think it was anything to do with a ring but, as her mother said, it did show good intent.

Of course, if Charlie had been an officer, it might have been different. Eileen Wilkins was engaged to an officer in the Royal Electrical and Mechanical Engineers. It wasn't that there was anything wrong about not being an officer, but now that the end of the war was in sight, as her mother said, there were going to be a lot of new values ...

Momentous events, Lobby Ludd was aware, always travelled in threes, but the third seemed reluctant to present itself. The letter from Freda Harris had immediately generated in him a sense of joyous reprieval. He wrote back forgiving all, and then won three successive games of cribbage against the stoker in the next bed, who had only one eye. It was later that he began to experience a feeling of not belonging.

He shrugged it aside. What he needed was a ship and the camaraderie of a mess-deck — any mess-deck, but the aftermess of LCF49 would do. He had no knowledge of the ship's movements since he had come ashore, but it was unlikely that she had returned to the Normandy beaches, from which the invasion fleets were dispersing. Harbours had been captured — Cherbourg, Dieppe, Le Havre and even Antwerp. Only the Schelde estuary remained to be prised open, and hundreds of landing ships and assault craft had already returned to UK bases to discharge their crews and then be moored, empty and rusting, in rivers and creeks along every coast. A number might be refitted and crewed for the long voyage to the Far East as a token contribution towards the Americans' final offensive, and LCF49 might be among that number; on the other hand, Lobby Ludd might be boarding her only in time for her last brief journey to a breaker's yard.

Lobby Ludd had been fit for duty, and feeling increasingly pessimistic, for several weeks when the third momentous event occurred. It was a drafting instruction that required him to rejoin LCF49, reporting in the first instance, for onward direction, to the naval transit authority in Lowestoft. Lowestoft? Shave off, wasn't that where the skipper lived?

How, or why, LCF49 had removed herself from Portsmouth to Lowestoft was a question he was not prepared to debate. He lashed his hammock and packed his kitbag, collected his travel warrant and draft chit, and a bag meal that he consigned to a waste bin on Portsmouth Station.

He had not travelled ashore for several months, and he was unprepared for the subtle changes that anticipation of the war's end had imposed.

Victory over Germany was no longer a distant, even debatable, possibility; it had become inevitable. It had become like a long card game in which the last few cards remained to be played, but with the Allies holding the trumps and both sides knowing it. Among the civil population there was an increasing air of impatience, even petulance, and the homespun strategists were in full cry as they had not been since the first few months of the war. There was, Lobby Ludd detected, already a hardening of attitudes, and he began to understand what Freda Harris had meant by a lot of new standards. But they were not new standards; they were the old ones returning. In the station buffet there was no wink and a glass of beer for a laden sailor. It was out of hours and would he not obstruct the door with his kitbag? A railway inspector scrutinized his travel warrant, grunted that he would be bloody glad when these things were finished with, and thrust it back. At Waterloo no porter shouted for him to throw his baggage on a trolley, and Liverpool Street was worse. Servicemen were a nuisance to the travelling public, and the public was beginning to put the serviceman in his rightful place. The Lowestoft train was crowded, and he met a battery of resentful eyes at the first compartment door he opened. 'Well,' he heard someone say as he closed it, 'we pay for our seats, don't we?'

*

In Lowestoft, at least, there was a salty smell, fishing-nets spread, ships' masts, and the sea. He never thought he'd be glad to see the 'ogwash. Well, not exactly glad. There were tank landing craft clustered against the jetties, but he could not see the familiar, ugly shape of an LCF.

At the office of NOIC a Wren petty officer was applying crimson varnish to her nails and did not remove her eyes from them as she spoke. LCF49? She shrugged. There were so many dirty little ships coming and going. No, NOIC had gone for the day, and he could report here again at 0900 tomorrow. Where should he go in the meantime? She splayed her fingers and frowned at them. Well, it really wasn't her concern, but she believed there was a seamen's hostel in Lowestoft. She was not sure where, but he could ask. No, he could not leave his bag and hammock here; this was an office, not a baggage store. And, no, there were no arrangements for issuing mismusters' rum.

Lobby Ludd located the seamen's hostel, reserved a bed on payment in advance of four shillings, and thankfully deposited the kitbag, hammock and suitcase he had wrestled with for hours. Kitbags ought to have bleedin' wheels on. The seamen's rest, a draughty warren of small cubicles, each containing a narrow bed, a chair, an enamel chamber-pot and a hook behind the door, was no place in which to remain unnecessarily, and he sought the jetty again.

It was darkening, with a chill November dampness that he could almost taste. He walked the length of the harbour wall, crossed the bridge, and continued walking slowly, hands in pockets and shoulders hunched. Several times he heard the music and voices of a bar beyond blackout curtains, but ignored them. He felt very lonely, but did not want the company of strangers.

It was eight o' clock. The last dog-watchmen would be coming below for supper, dragging off their oilskins and blowing on cold fingers. Liver an' onions? Shave off. Did yer say liver or leather? Pass the salt, Bowlesey. Why are we the only mess with a soddin' pea in the butter? Yer Bleedin' lucky, mate. I knew a bloke that found a toe in his shepherd's pie. The cook said so what? It proved it was genuine ...

Lobby Ludd halted. He must have been walking, deep in thought, for twenty minutes. He was on the sea road, and he could just see the white of crawling surf fifty yards distant, beyond the dark foreshore, and hear the hiss of shingle. It was cold, and the wind was rising.

He shrugged himself into his collar, turned to retrace his steps, then halted again. The tiniest glimmer of light came from a window only a few paces away. There were other windows, darkened and silent, a low roof, and a sign that hung over a porched door. The Lifeboat.

It could be what he needed for an hour — a quiet bar and a fire. He pushed open the door and entered.

There was a floor of polished tiles, a deep fireplace in which burned a basket of logs, chairs with cushions, pewter, several vases of flowers. The bar counter, against the far wall, was tiny, and he could see only half a dozen bottles on a tray. There were no other customers. This, he supposed, was what they called a lounge, which meant saloon-bar prices and don't drop fag-ends on the carpet. He walked to the fire and spread out his hands. Above him, on the wall, was a picture of a lifeboat under oars, ploughing through a tempestuous sea towards a foundered sailing ship. Beneath it was the legend, 'Caister Men Never Turn Back.'

'I ain't surprised,' he said aloud, 'if they were staying at the Mission ter Seamen.'

'Can I help you?' enquired a quiet voice from behind him, and he turned.

She was of medium height, slim, with brushed, dark hair tied on her neck in a small club, and her eyes were large in a well-boned face palely free of cosmetics. She was oldish, Lobby Ludd assessed; she must be all of twenty-eight, but he had seen her kind among the pages of the Tatler and Country Life — those thoroughbred women who could wear old tweeds or corduroys with the same easy grace as a silk gown at the Ritz. She was not his idea of a barmaid; she must be the guv'nor's wife.

'I'd like a pint o' bitter, miss,' he said, 'if yer've got bitter.'

She frowned very slightly and did not move for several moments, as if debating some sudden question. Then, 'Yes,' she nodded, and went to the bar. Her feet were silent on the tiles.

He heard the chink of bottles. 'We seem to have only Pale Ale,' she declared. 'Is that the same as bitter?'

Lobby Ludd chuckled. 'I thought yer was going ter say yer only 'ad shandies. It ain't 'xactly the same, but it's better'n — ' He stopped. 'It'll be fine, miss.'

She brought it carefully to him. 'I hope you don't mind a pewter pot. It's got a glass bottom.'

He tried to think of something witty to say about a glass bottom, but could not. 'How much is that, miss?'

The frown came again, and several more seconds elapsed before she replied, 'How much is it usually?'

This, he decided, was a bleedin' comical pub. 'It depends,' he said. 'Usually elevenpence in the public, a shilling in the saloon. Unless it's Bass. That's another penny.'

She considered. 'Elevenpence, then.'

He reached into a pocket, but there was something indefinably, uncomfortably wrong about everything. He glanced up at her, at the chairs, the cushions, the vases of chrysanthemums, then back at her. For a fleeting moment the gravity had gone from her eyes, and they were warm, mischief-filled. The truth burst like a thunder-clap.

'Shave-off,' he swallowed. 'This ain't a pub.'

She shook her head and smiled. 'No.'

'Shave off,' he repeated stupidly, and fumbled for his cap. 'I'm sorry. I thought I saw a sign outside — '

'You did.' She lifted a hand. 'No, please don't go. Please have your drink — on the house.' She smiled again. 'Fifty years ago this was a lifeboat station, until the sea-wall was built, which meant the boat couldn't be launched. It was all done manually in those days. It became a small inn — the Lifeboat — but I think it was never very prosperous, being so remote. It's been a private house since the war began. We — my husband and I — kept the old sign hanging, but if it had not been dark you would have seen the notice, "Private", on the gate.'

'I didn't even see the gate,' Lobby Ludd confessed. He gazed at her. She was, he was beginning to realize, bleedin' smashing, even if she was all of twenty-eight. 'Ain't it a bit risky, leaving the door unlocked? I mean,' he hastened to assure her, 'I'm all right, but there's some that ain't. Is your husband — ?'

Her eyes moved in the direction of the door, but they looked far beyond to horizons of her own. 'We never locked the door,' she said very quietly. 'The lifeboat station was never locked, so that the first men to arrive could reach the boat. For us it seemed wrong to lock the door — and I shall never lock it now.' Lobby Ludd decided to say nothing. He wanted to look at her because she was such a smasher, but it was ill-mannered to stare. He sipped his beer and stole a glance over the rim of his tankard. 'Do sit down,' she invited, and he did. 'What is your name? Is your ship in Lowestoft?'

'Ludd,' he confided. Now he could gaze directly at her, and knew exactly what love at first sight really meant. This was what it was. All the others had been cheap little pushers compared with this wonderful creature. 'I've jes' come from Portsmouth,' he went on, 'ter rejoin my ship — LCF49 — but she ain't 'ere.'

Then he saw the remaining colour drain from her face and her lip quiver. Her eyes were wider than ever, and he tried frantically to think what he had said that was so shocking. Ludd, he'd said, that was all.

'Ludd,' she whispered. 'You're Lobby Ludd.'

He grinned, relieved. 'And yer can claim the News Chronicle prize.' He had heard it so many times during his young life that, usually, it no longer drew more than a grunt from him, but she could say it as often as she liked.

'And you don't know?' she asked. 'They haven't told you?'

'Where LCF49 is? No. I ain't seen anyone that knows, yet. I jes' hope I don't 'ave ter lug my bag and 'ammock all the way back ter Poole or Plymouth, that's all.'

The room was very quiet, and they could just hear the rustle of the surf beyond the window. Suddenly she sank to her knees at his elbow. 'You were the bunting-topper,' she told him.

He was surprised. 'Bunting-tosser,' he corrected, nodding. 'Well, I still am, I'ope.'

He studied the frothed surface of his beer; she was alarmingly near, and he sat very still. She smelled nice, too. It was funny, he thought, how the classy ones always smelled nicer than the others. It was a bleedin' good job he'd had a haircut last Tuesday, and he'd shaved at the Mission to Seamen.

'Please,' she said, 'tell me about LCF49. Everything you can remember.'

Everything about LCF49? What for? He placed his tankard down, surprised, and she guiltily climbed to her feet. 'I'm sorry — you're almost empty. I'll get you more — or would you prefer something different?'

He was embarrassed. 'No, miss — ma'am — I mean, beer's fine, thanks — '

She refilled his tankard with the painstaking exactness of the inexpert, then lowered herself again to her knees at the chair-side. 'Now,' she begged.

'Well,' he frowned, 'she ain't much ter get excited about; I can think of a lot o' ships that's prettier. Take the cruiser Daemon that I was in, fer a start, or Virtue — she was a V & W destroyer — '

'No,' she insisted, and placed a gentle hand on his forearm, 'LCF49.'

So Lobby Ludd told her about LCF49, her ugly shape and the soot from the galley chimney, the big diesel engines that kept the plates dancing on the mess-tables, and the close-slung hammocks swinging against the deck-head. He told her about Perk and Walt, and Peach being sick in the Christmas nuts, Lieutenant Turk's tartan slippers and ERA Gilbert's size twelve shoes. She listened in silence, her eyes never leaving his face, but occasionally he sensed that she nodded, and her gaze became distant, as if he was merely reminding her of something she had heard before.

Three times, as he talked, a clock chimed, but she ignored it. When he mentioned the assault on Juno beach her hand moved to his arm again, and remained there, and she smiled gently, almost reminiscently, when he spoke of the bent rudder shaft and the weeks of K-ration tea.

He told her briefly of the struggle in the sea with the explosive motor-boat, suggesting that the adventure shared with Lieutenant Turk was one of slapstick comedy rather than of desperate peril. She was not deceived, but remained unspeaking while he described the exchange with the E-boat, the arrival of Toreador and the shelling by the shore battery.

He reached for his beer. 'And then you were injured,' she concluded.

The tankard had not reached his lips. He stared at her, surprised; he had said nothing about being injured.

'You must have been,' she added quickly, confused for the first time, 'or you would not have been left ashore.' Her eyes begged that he should not dispute it, and he did not. 'That's right', he agreed, aware now that something was happening that he did not understand.

She rose. 'Would you like some sandwiches or coffee?' Lobby Ludd glanced at his watch, amazed that it was almost midnight. He'd like coffee, he said, and then he must go. The door of the seamen's hostel would be locked, and he would have to knock up a bad-tempered night porter. It was funny how night porters were always bad-tempered. His eyes followed her thoughtfully as she left the room.

The probable irascibility of a night porter was of small consequence. He glanced around him again for some answer to the several questions he would have liked to ask her, but lacked the courage because, inexplicably, he did not wish to hear the answers. The room told him nothing.

He rose when she reappeared, and she placed the coffee on a small table. Then she drew a deep breath and faced him. 'You don't have to return to the seamen's hostel tonight. You can stay here,' she paused. 'No, don't say anything. I want you to stay here, with me. It's all I have to give you, but I owe it, because you sent someone back to me — if only for a short while. And I want to pretend, just once more. It's important to me, more than you can possibly understand ... '

He had never imagined, ever, that it could be like this. In the darkness she was soft and warm, trembling at the first, tentative touch of his fingers, but she responded quickly, and demanded with lips and arms and thighs with all the urgency of one long denied or shamelessly wanting. He would not have believed, earlier, that the quiet-voiced woman with the big, sad eyes who had knelt demurely at his elbow could be the eager, female animal who clung to him with all her panting strength, and then, in one incandescent moment, cried out a name that was not his, but which he remembered. He was exhausted before her, and slept with his cheek against her breasts, her fingers stroking his hair as she stared into the darkness with tear-filled eyes, listening to the distant sea.

*

It was morning when he awoke; she had gone from the bed, but he could near her moving below. He found the bathroom, then dressed, and descended. She was preparing breakfast in the kitchen, and gave him a quick smile from the stove, saying nothing.

He sat at a table alone, but she shared a pot of strong tea with him. She preferred strong tea to coffee for breakfast, she said, and hoped he did not mind. It was going to be a cold, sunny day, and the sea calm. A good day for the drifters out of Lowestoft. She stood as he ate, with both hands clasped around her cup, her hair hidden, peasant-like, under a colourful, tied kerchief. There was nothing in her manner to hint that last night had ever happened.

The moment had to come, and he rose to his feet. 'I never thought, when I came in, that this would 'appen,' he began, but she raised a finger.

'It's not for either of us to talk about, Lobby Ludd, only to remember sometimes, if you think it's worth remembering. We shall never see each other again, and if you are the fine person I think you are you'll never whisper a word, or try to know more.' She stood at the door as he walked away on the empty road that was still shining with morning wetness, and he did not glance back.

*

At the office of NOIC the Wren petty officer was studying her teeth with the aid of a small mirror, and told him to wait, which was predictable. He waited while she squeezed a spot on her chin and combed her hair. Her toilet satisfactorily completed, she picked up a telephone to speak to the inner room. 'There's no urgency, sir,' he heard her say. 'It's only the rating who arrived yesterday for LCF49. Will you have your coffee first?'

The telephone in her hand spat angrily, and she flushed. 'I'm sorry, sir — I only thought — ' She glared at Lobby Ludd. 'You can go in. Have you wiped your feet?'

'Leading Signalman Ludd.' The Lieutenant-Commander looked up from the draft note, put his tongue into a cheek and narrowed his eyes. 'For LCF49.' There was something wrong, Lobby Ludd knew. 'I'm sorry you drew a blank yesterday. I know what that seamen's hostel is like — as cold as charity and smelling of damp plaster.'

He frowned at the draft note. 'I'm afraid, Ludd that you've had a journey for nothing. I don't know why the drafting office did it, unless it was because you were earmarked for rejoining some time ago, and nobody checked further. The fact is Ludd' — he paused — 'that there's no LCF49 for you to rejoin.'

'You mean she's gone, sir?' He might have bleedin' known it. It was just his bleedin' luck.

'Gone? Yes, Ludd,' the other nodded. 'She should have returned to Lowestoft after the Walcheren landing of last week — 1 November — only she didn't. You've read about the Walcheren landing?' He nodded again. 'Lieutenant Turk and his wife were friends of mine, and I got a copy of the official report for her. Would you like to hear it?' He took up a paper. '"Despite supporting fire from Warspite and two monitors the landing operation was met by heavy shore battery fire. Notwithstanding, the assault squadron of twenty-five craft pressed home its attack. Nine vessels were sunk before reaching the dyke and eleven others put out of action. LCF49, commanded by Lieutenant Samuel Turk, RNR, was deliberately run ashore to engage German positions at point-blank range. This gallant action distracted the enemy sufficiently to allow commandos of the 4th Special Brigade to land on both shoulders of the Westkapelle Gap almost unopposed, and the beachhead was successfully established. The LCF bore the full brunt of enemy artillery fire, and there were no survivors."'

Lobby Ludd made no comment. The Lieutenant-Commander glanced up, misinterpreting the silence. 'I'd say they did pretty well, wouldn't you, Ludd?'

'Pretty well?' Lobby Ludd stared. 'They're bleedin' dead, ain't they? How can being dead be doing pretty well? I mean, what 'appens when yer do pretty bad?'

'I'll make you out a travel warrant for Devonport Barracks,' the officer decided, reaching for a pen. 'It's odd that LCF49 should have sailed from Lowestoft, but lucky in a way. Lieutenant Turk and his wife lived here for several years — did you know that? They had an old house on the sea road — the Lifeboat.' His head was lowered. 'I imagine you'll be glad to get back into General Service. These Combined Operations craft will soon be back numbers.'

*

Lobby Ludd descended the steps into the street, unseeing. It was suddenly cold, and he shivered. There was a soddin' lot of back numbers, mate — the broken hulks that lay off the beaches of Normandy and the Dutch dykes, rusted in Dieppe harbour, at Salerno and Anzio. Yer could bet, in time, there'd be a book of names, under glass, in the barracks drill shed, with a page turned every day if someone remembered. Perhaps, sometimes, blokes waiting to muster for duty watch would read the names of ships like Hood, and Repulse, and Prince of Wales — the ships that soddin' history was written about. But what, they'd wonder, was bleedin' LCF49?

He walked to the jetty's edge, gazed at the shabby craft moored alongside and in mid-river, deserted and silent. They were all back numbers. He buttoned the neck of his coat. One day, mate, he resolved, he'd write a soddin' book, that's what.

Glossary of Naval Lower-deck Terminology and Technical Terms

Many naval expressions have passed into common use and their original meanings have become blurred. Many others, from sailing-ship days, have passed into misuse. Those listed below were common during the Second World War, and undoubtedly some survive.

The list is, of course, by no means complete, but expressions and abbreviations used in the text are included, together with one or two others which give the flavour of the period.

Nicknames have not been included because they were so numerous. A Williams was inevitably a 'Bungy', Wilson a 'Tug', Bell a 'Dinger' and every Knight a 'Bogey'. Ships also had their nicknames. Royal Sovereign was the 'Tiddley Quid', Vengeance was the 'Lord's Own' ('Vengeance is Mine, saith the Lord. I will repay') and Weston-super-Mare became 'Aggie on Horseback' — a subtlety that the reader can unravel for himself by referring to the notation against 'Aggie Weston'.

*

AB Able Seaman

Active Service Term applied to ratings of the regular Navy although, contrarily, they were of peacetime recruitment.

adrift Late, particularly when mustering or returning from leave.

Aggie Weston Loosely applied to all seamen's temperance hostels ashore, but particularly those originally introduced by Dame Agnes Weston, the 'sailors' best friend', who, however, also persuaded the Admiralty to stop issuing rum to ratings of under twenty years.

all night in For watchkeeping sailors, the occasion on which they enjoyed an entire night in their hammocks. Ashore, all night abed with a woman.

Ally Sloper's Favourite Relish A particularly racy bottled sauce, available from the ship's stores, reputed to be excellent for cleaning brasswork.

Andrew [The] The lower deck's name for the Royal Navy. During the Napoleonic Wars, Andrew Miller was a notorious press-gang officer who impressed so many seamen that he was said to own the navy.

asdic Submarine-detection branch, equipment and techniques. From the initial letters of the Anti-Submarine Detection Investigation Committee of 1917.

ATS Auxiliary Territorial Service, former name of the Women's Royal Army Corps.

baby's head See 'dead baby'.

back teeth awash Drunken, or the process of becoming so.

BAMS Wireless broadcast service for British and Allied merchant ships.

baron One with modest accumulation of money, usually by saving, and a target for borrowers.

battle-wagon Battleship.

bear pit The stokers' mess-deck.

belay Stop or cancel. To 'belay the last pipe' would be a cancellation of the last order given.

bells Bell-bottomed trousers, sometimes worn extravagantly wide in defiance of regulations.

Blue Label Popular brand of bottled beer, brewed in Malta.

Bluenose One who has travelled north of the Arctic Circle. Circumstances permitting, first-timers are subjected to a light-hearted ceremony similar to that when crossing the Equator, and presented with a 'Bluenose certificate' signed by the ship's captain.

BN Continuous wireless broadcast for warships, 107 kc/s.

boatswain's pipe A whistle blown by boatswain or quartermaster to precede orders given to crew or watch, or as a salute to senior officer or another ship. Today, most orders or announcements are broadcast over the ship's amplifier system.

Bootnecks Royal Marines, for whom sailors had little affection.

breathing licence Station card — an identity card held by all ratings, deprival of which meant loss of leave and limitation of leisure activities.

bubbly Rum, issued to eligible ratings daily.

Buffer; Chief Buffer Bosun's Mate; Chief Bosun's Mate.

bulkheads The dividing walls of below-decks compartments.

bunting General term for flags of all kinds.

bunting-tosser, Bunts Rating of Visual Signalling Branch.
buzz Rumour, often distorted by repetition or completely unfounded,
buzzer Closed-circuit morse code for practice purposes.
BWO Bridge Wireless Office.
cable [length] Unit of distance, about 200 yards.
Captain D Senior officer of destroyer flotilla.
Carley floats Life rafts of varying sizes, often made of balsa.
caterer Senior rating in mess, once responsible for victualling arrangements.
Charlie [Chaplin] Ship's chaplain, Padre.
Chinese wedding-cake Boiled rice, laced with currents.
Chippy Ship's carpenter.
chocker Fed up, frustrated. Abbreviation of 'chocka-block', meaning a rope that is jammed tightly into its block.
civvies Civilian clothes.
Civvy Street Civilian life, the yearned-for end of a service engagement.
clacker Pastry or pie crust.
cleaning station Appointed location for daily cleaning duties.
clew up Finish, end up. A defaulter might 'clew up' in gaol.
coaming Vertical erection around hatch or at base of door to prevent entrance of water.
Cook of the Mess Rating(s) responsible for bringing food from galley, washing up, cleaning mess-decks.
corned dog Corned beef.
cowboys Bacon and beans.
crusher Regulating Petty Officer (RPO), member of naval police branch, allegedly the last resort of the moronic or illiterate.
daymen Ratings who do no watchkeeping and work during day hours only, thus enjoying 'all night in' every night.
DD tanks Dual-drive amphibious tanks, with engines driving both tracks and marine screws.
dead baby Sometimes 'baby's head'. Meat pudding.
deckhead The ceiling of any below-deck area.
depot Devonport, Portsmouth and Chatham were depots, also port divisions to one of which every rating belonged, defined by the letter D, P or C prefixing his official number.

DFs Duty Frees, referring to duty-free cigarettes or tobacco.
D/F Direction finding.
dhobeying The process of washing clothes.
dickie White linen bib-like item, secured by tapes, worn instead of a standard seaman's shirt.
Dip, at the 'At the dip!' was a response when addressed or called; an acknowledgement. An ensign was dipped in salute or acknowledgement of another.
ditty box Small box of scrubbed white wood, with brass name-plate and lock, in which a rating kept his most private possessions, letters, photographs, etc. divisions Morning muster of ship's company.
DNO Director of Naval Operations.
DO Divisional Officer, of which there might be a number in a ship, each responsible for different professional branches.
draft chit Drafting instructions to or from a ship or foreign station
drills White drill uniform.
drink, the sea, particularly that in close proximity; e.g., ' ... fell into the drink'.
ducks See 'Number Threes' for definitions of naval kit.
EA Electrical Artificer.
E-boat German, diesel-engined, high speed torpedo launch, the counterpart of the British Motor Torpedo Boat (qv), but larger, more seaworthy, and more heavily armed. Displacement 93 tons.
EDR Electrical Distance Recorder.
ENSA Entertainment National Service Association; a wartime organization providing travelling concert parties for the armed services.
ERA Engine Room Artificer.
ETA Estimated Time of Arrival.
fearnought Stout, felt worsted cloth, fire-resistant, once used for stokers' trousers but more latterly to re-inforce damage-control plugs and for fire-fighting.
Fill your boots! Help yourself!
filled in Suffer bruises or beating in fight or brawl.
fish-heads Aircraft carrier's ship's company, as opposed to Fleet Air Arm personnel. (See 'pin-heads'.)
flakers Exhausted. To 'flake out' is to collapse.

flannel (1) Seamen's white flannel shirt, with square-cut neck edged with blue jean. (2) Nonsense, unconvincing bluster.

flat aback Cap worn on back of head, contrary to regulations.

flunkey Officer's servant or steward.

foo-foo Talcum powder, used to limit perspiration and prickly heat, sometimes violently scented.

fore and aft rig Naval uniform involving peaked cap, jacket, and trousers creased at front and back.

gannet One with a voracious or greedy appetite,

gash Refuse or garbage. This must be disposed of with caution in wartime as it can betray a ship's presence to a submarine, and discarded written material may impart useful information.

Gestapo Regulating Branch personnel.

goofers Idlers and off-duty men who congregate to watch some interesting procedure, sometimes in hazardous circumstances.

green rub Misfortune, an undeserved penalty.

groundbait Small gift, such as stockings or cosmetics, given to female acquaintance, with ulterior motive.

guard and steerage Watchkeepers and other personnel with arduous duties who are allowed extra sleep periods and other privileges.

gulpers A gulp of another's tot of rum, conceded as payment for some service, or as a gambling debt. (See 'sippers'.)

Gut Notorious street of bars and places of entertainment in Valetta, Malta, riotously frequented by sailors.

Guzz Devonport depot, dockyard and barracks. When affiliated to the Devenport port division, a man is a 'Guzz rating'.

HA High Angle, with particular reference to high-angle anti-aircraft guns.

hard liers Small bonus once paid in compensation for the hard conditions of small ships.

HD Continuous wireless broadcast for warships, 78 Kc/s. See also 'BN'.

HE High Explosive; also Hydrophone Effect.

heads Latrines, in earlier times always in the head, or bows, of a ship.

Hedgerow A multiple weapon consisting of 24 mortars, installed in minor landing craft and intended for the explosion of beach minefields in the path of invading forces.

herrings-in Tinned herrings in tomato sauce, a frequent breakfast dish.
H/F High Frequency.
HO 'Hostilities Only'; a rating conscripted for the duration of hostilities.
hogwash [hoggin'] Sea, sea water.
homers A domestic environment ashore, not necessarily a rating's own home, which he visits. He is then said to be 'up 'omers'.
Hooky Term of address for a leading rating, identified by an anchor badge on his left arm.
Jack Dusty Rating of the Stores Branch; any rating employed in storekeeping.
Jack Strop Belligerent or impertinent rating.
jankers Punishment routine imposed on defaulters.
Jaunty Master-at-Arms, senior rating of naval police branch and probably the most unpopular person in any ship or establishment.
Jimmy, Jimmy the One First Lieutenant, responsible for the smooth running of ship's routine and daily work-programme. See also 'Number One'.
joss Luck. Bad joss in bad luck, misfortune.
kedge Anchor. To kedge a vessel is to move it by laying out an anchor and then heaving her up to it.
Kil' 'Kil'-class patrol sloop, a class with names beginning with 'Kil', e.g., Kilburnie, Kilkenzie, Kilmore, etc. killick Leading rating of any branch; e.g., killick sparker, killick of the mess, etc.
KR and AI King's Regulations and Admiralty Instructions.
KUA Kit Upkeep Allowance; a small supplement to cover the replacement of uniform kit which, after the first issue, must be purchased by the rating.
kye Cocoa, made from solid bricks of unsweetened chocolate which must be grated or crushed before adding hot water.
lamp swinging Boastful reminiscing.
lamps trimmed Suffer injury or punishment in fight or brawl.
L and PA Lodging and Provision Allowance. Additional payment to ratings who are quartered in private accommodation ashore.
LCA Landing Craft Assault. Launches of about 40 feet length, for beach landing, accommodating 35 troops (or 800 lbs equipment) and a naval crew of 4.

LCF(L) Landing Craft Flak. Close support vessel equipped with large number of medium-calibre guns for use against aircraft or for near-range bombardment of enemy fortifications. Complement 70.

LCG(L) Landing Craft Gun. Similar to LCF, but with two 4.7-inch guns. Complement 50.

LCT(L) Landing Craft Tank. Vessel purpose-built for the transport and beach-landing of tanks and other vehicles. They varied in displacement up to 350 tons unladen, and typical loads would be five 40-ton tanks, or eleven at 30 tons, or ten 3-ton trucks, or 300 tons deadweight.

N.B. Letters in parentheses, i.e., (L), (M), or (S), indicate Large, Medium or Small versions of the vessel class.

liberty boat (occasionally a road vehicle) taking men ashore for leave.

Lobs! Peculiar to Boys' Service, a shout of warning at the approach of danger, e.g., an officer or instructor.

LST Landing Ship Tank. Ocean-going transports with hinged ramp in bows, capable of discharging tanks and other vehicles on to open beaches. Displacements ranging from 2,000 to 5,000 tons.

main brace, splice the To splice the main brace is to issue an extra tot of rum to all hands, usually as a reward following action or a particularly hard period of work. Originally, the main brace, one of the thickest and heaviest ropes in a ship, was spliced only very occasionally.

make-and-mend A period of no duties, usually a half day, originally given to seamen for the purpose of making and mending clothes, but in more recent times for sleeping, shore-going or recreation.

Maltese Lace Ragged or holed clothing, particularly underclothing.

matelot Lower-deck sailor.

mess-deck lawyer The equivalent of a barrackroom lawyer; one able to quote chapter and verse of regulations.

mess-traps Crockery and utensils used on mess-decks.

Mickey Mouse Motor Mechanic (naval), from the initials MM.

mismusters' issue of rum at end of day for those ratings who missed the scheduled midday issue, usually because of absence ashore on duty or travel.

ML Motor Launch.

M/L Minelayer.

MTB Motor Torpedo Boat. Petrol-engined, high-speed launch, of which there were many variations, but most carrying two torpedoes and modest anti-aircraft weapons.

muzzle velocity Tinned meat and vegetables, from the initials M & V.

nap hand Venereal Disease.

Navvy Navigating Officer.

neaters Rum issued undiluted (neat) as opposed to grog, which has water added, and is classified as one-and-one, two-and-one, etc.

Nife lamp Emergency, battery-fed lamp, switched on either manually or automatically when mains electricity supply fails.

NOIC Naval Officer in Charge; the resident naval authority in most seaports.

north-easter Stoppage of pay, from the initials 'NE' in the pay ledger, meaning 'not entitled', and imposing a cold wind of poverty.

nozzer A recently enlisted boy; a raw recruit.

Number One First Lieutenant. See 'Jimmy the One'.

Number Threes A rating's third-best blue suit. A full kit should include four blue suits, numbered one to four; number fives, white ducks; number six, white drills — through working rigs, overalls, tropical shorts, etc. The 'rig for the day' is specified daily, or for certain duties. Only 'number ones' has gold badges.

nutty Any kind of sweetmeat or confection. The terms 'chocolate*, 'toffee', etc., are almost never used.

OA Ordnance Artificer.

OD Ordinary Rating; the lowest rating in men's service.

'Oggie Hot cornish pastry, often eaten ashore or in canteen, particularly in Devonport.

onion A fraction of a knot (nautical measurement of speed). Thus 'ten knots and an onion' would mean something between ten and eleven knots. One knot is a speed of 2,000 yards, a nautical mile, per hour.

OOD Officer of the Day.

OOW Officer of the Watch.

oppo Friend or shore-going companion, from 'opposite number'.

Out pipes Order given to indicate a resumption of work, or shortly before night retirement. Originally meaning that tobacco pipes should be extinguished.

party Any woman, but usually an acquaintance, casual or formal.

Pay Bob Paymaster.

paid off On completion of a commission, possibly of several years, a ship returned to its home port and 'paid off' its company, who returned to depot to await further drafting.

pea doo Pea soup.

pierhead jump Orders to join a ship at extremely short notice.

pigs Officers.

pin-heads Fleet Air Arm personnel, as opposed to ship's company, in aircraft carrier.

Pipe down Order imposing silence, the last routine order of the day, following 'out pipes'.

P/L Plain Language, as opposed to code or cipher.

Pompey Portsmouth depot, dockyard and barracks. Men affiliated to the Portsmouth port division are 'Pompey ratings'.

pom-pom Two-pounder Maxim gun, for both high and low-angle firing.

pongo Soldier.

pusher Woman, usually one of casual acquaintance.

pusser Corruption of 'purser', denoting any item of service issue, whether food, clothing or equipment; the word also describes anything that is correct or conforming to regulations. A 'pusser' ship or person is one that is strict and highly disciplined.

QF Quick Firing.

rabbits Gifts or souvenirs, usually purchased ashore, intended for family or friends at home. A 'rabbit run' is an excursion ashore primarily for the purpose of gift-buying.

rate of knots At high speed. Any journey or activity undertaken speedily is said to be done 'at a rate of knots'.

rattle, in the Faced with disciplinary action.

RDF Radio Direction Finding, by which the bearing of a ship's radio transmission can be determined.

red ink A character assessment of 'Excellent', which is written in records in red ink. More normal assessments, in black ink, were 'Very Good', 'Good' or merely 'Satisfactory'.

requestmen Men submitting a request (for leave, advancement etc.) through official channels. They were interviewed prior to, but on the same occasion as, defaulters.

RNB Royal Naval Barracks.

Roll on my twelve! Frequent **cri de coeur**, referring to the longed-for expiry of a service engagement, of twelve years or any other period.

Rose Cottage The Venereal Diseases ward in Sick Quarters.

rounds Inspection of ship or establishment by duty officer during late evening; captain's rounds occurred during Saturday forenoons, following an intensive cleaning programme.

round turn To be 'brought up with a round turn' is to be dramatically halted or foiled, as a running rope is when turned, or looped, around a bollard.

Royals Royal Marines.

R/T Radio Telephony. Voice transmissions, as opposed to morse code (W/T).

rum bosun Rating in mess responsible for collecting and distributing rum issue.

rum rat One with insatiable appetite for rum, both his own and others'.

salt horse An officer of solely seamanship qualifications, as opposed to those with specialist training, e.g., communications, flying, torpedoes, gunnery, etc.

Saturday night sailors Officers and ratings of the Royal Naval Volunteer Reserve.

Sally The The Salvation Army.

SBA Sick Berth Attendant.

SBNO Senior British Naval Officer.

scran bag All items of clothing and kit left unstowed were confiscated and put into a 'scran bag'. They were subsequently redeemed by their owners on payment of an inch of soap for each item. The soap was used for common cleaning purposes.

scribe Writer; rating on the navy's clerical branch.

scrub round Ignore, cancel, or take no further action.

SDO Signal Distribution Office.

set A beard, for the growth of which it was necessary to obtain official permission.

shave off To shave off beard, the removal of which must also be officially approved. Also, the expression 'Shave off!' indicated surprise, frustration or disgust.

shite hawks Seagulls, unpopular for their depredation of paintwork and polished brass.

shamfered Damaged. A ship suffering damage in action was said to have been 'shamfered'.

shock To cook. A dish taken to the galley would be accompanied by a request to 'give it a shock'.

short arm inspection Medical Officer's examination of genitals.

sippers A sip of another's rum, conceded as payment for favour or gambling debt. Two sippers equalled one gulpers.

skate Rating with a bad disciplinary record, spending frequent periods under punishment.

slops Items of uniform kit purchased from ship's stores; pusser's issue.

Smoke, The London.

snottie Midshipman, who wears three brass buttons on each cuff, allegedly to prevent them being used to wipe nose.

sparker, Sparks Telegraphist Rating.

spin a yarn To tell a story in defence of misdemeanour to deceive by verbosity; boastful reminiscence.

Spithead Pheasant Kipper.

sprog Infant; anyone of immature years.

square rig Naval uniform involving blue jean collar, jumper and bell-bottomed trousers.

squeegee band Improvised musical group, utilizing mouth organs, combs, clappers and unusual percussion media.

SRE Sound Reproduction Equipment, for amplifying orders throughout ship, and for radio programmes.

stanchion Rating who has held a comfortable shore posting for unusually long time.

stand easy Brief cessation of work during forenoon and afternoon, usually giving time for a smoke and cup of tea.

station card Small identity card held by all ratings, withdrawn during loss of leave or other privileges.

Stokes Stoker.

stone frigate Any naval barracks or shore establishment.

Stringbag Swordfish torpedo-carrying biplane.

Stripey Rating with three good-conduct badges (stripes) indicating lengthy service and particularly one who has achieved no promotion. They represent at least thirteen years 'undetected crime'.

stroppy Belligerent, insubordinate. The description of a 'Jack Strop'.

Sub Variously, a sub-lieutenant, a submarine, a loan of money,

swing the lamp To relate or boast of harrowing seafaring experiences, at which a listener might scoff, 'Swing the lamp', tailor-made Manufactured cigarette, as opposed to one rolled by hand.

TBS Radiotelephone for 'Talk Between Ships'.

T, G, or UA Temperance, Grog, or Under Age. A rating is Under Age until twenty, when he may opt to draw rum (in which case he is defined as 'G') or to draw a small payment in lieu (and so become 'T'). A temperance rating as a rara avis,

three-badger See 'Stripey'.

ticket Discharge from the service. To get one's ticket was an enviable achievement.

tickler Cigarette and pipe tobacco allowance, packed in 1/2lb tins, a duty-free purchase. A hand-rolled cigarette was also a 'tickler'. The name comes from that of a manufacturer of tinned jam.

tiddley Neat, or of good appearance. Applied equally to the tie of a cap ribbon, the cut of a suit, or the lines of a ship.

tiffy Artificer, either Engine Room, Ordnance or Electrical.

tiller flat Aftermost compartment of ship, housing emergency steering position and, when applicable, depth-charge stowage.

tinfish Torpedo.

tombola The Naval equivalent of 'Bingo'.

Torps Torpedo officer or rating.

tot Measure of rum issued to eligible ratings daily, at midday. Rum is denied to defaulters.

Townie Specifically, another rating who originates from the same home town, but often used as a friendly form of address.

Uckers A complex version of the table game Ludo, widely played on mess-decks.

UJC Union Jack Club; servicemen's hostel near Waterloo Station.

'Up Spirits' The midday announcement indicating that rum is about to be issued, responded to by the 'rum bosun' of each mess, who draws the ration for his fellows. When the announcement is made a common riposte is 'And stand fast the Holy Ghost!'.

up the line To travel home on leave, as opposed to local leave ashore.

victualled To be officially listed for maintenance by a ship or mess, on permanent or temporary basis, so that accommodation, food and rum can be issued.

VAD Nursing auxiliary of the Voluntary Aid Detachment.

V/S Visual Signalling.

V & W A class of destroyer built between 1917 and 1919, all bearing names beginning with 'V', or 'W', and of which fifty-eight were in service in 1939.

watchkeepers' Extended shore leave and/or sleeping periods allowed to watchkeeping personnel in compensation for long working hours.

Wavy Navy Royal Naval Volunteer Reserve, from the wavy gold bands on the cuff of an RNVR officer which distinguish him from a colleague of the regular navy.

winger Chosen friend or shore-going companion.

W/T Wireless Telegraphy, generally assumed to mean morse code transmissions as opposed to voice telephony (R/T).

Printed in Great Britain
by Amazon